Lynton's
South African
Adventure:

Demon of Fire
at the
Karoo Escarpment

J. Wayne Frye

Canadian English is used in this book, so teachers should make students aware of the spelling differences. It is suggested that vocabulary (see back of book), which is organized by chapter, be reviewed prior to reading.

Lynton's South African Adventure: Demon of Fire at the Karoo Escarpment

THE AUTHOR

Wayne Frye's Girl series, Aaron Adams, Chablis Louise Chavez and Lynton books are popular among mystery readers. He writes satirical political commentary for newspapers and his books on politics have created a great deal of controversy. He has written marketing/advertising textbooks, been a highly successful U.S. university hockey coach, professor, university president and served as a marketing consultant to hockey teams and motion picture companies. He has been cited for his work with inner-city gang children in the Los Angeles area and been active in the anti-globalization movement. He lives in Ladysmith, British Columbia, Laguna, Philippines and Cape Town, South Africa.

Other Books by J. Wayne Frye

The author with the real Lynton Viñas

Worth
Pursuit
Lynton Curls Her Hair
Lynton Buys a New Cell-Phone
And Hears the Voice of Doom
Lynton Walks on Water
Fall From Apocalypse
Armageddon Now
Lynton and the Vampire at Tagaytay Manor
Lynton and the Ghosts in the Mansion on Balete Drive
Hockey Mania and the Mystery of Nancy Running Elk
Something Evil in the Darkness at Hopkins House
How Hockey Saved a Jew From the Holocaust:
The Rudi Ball Story
The Girl Who Stirred up the Whirlwind
The Girl Who Motivated Murder Most Foul
The Girl Who Said Goodbye for the Last Time
When Jesus Came to Jersey as the Son of Thunder
When Jesus Came to Canada to Lead an Indigenous Rebellion
Canadian Angels of Mercy – Nurses in Times of Peril
Points of Rebellion: Aboriginals Who Fought for Justice
Chablis and Lynton in the Room of Doom
Chablis: Avenging Angel for the Forgotten
In the City of Lost Hope
Chablis and the Terrorist Who Resurrected the Spirit of Che

Lynton's South African Adventure:
Demon of Fire at the Karoo Escarpment

TABLE OF CONTENTS

Lynton's South African Adventure:
Demon of Fire at the Karoo Escarpment

TO: Lynton's First South African Friend:
Thato

And to the man from
Tarzana, California
who inspired my initial interest in Africa
so many years ago,
Edgar Rice Burroughs.

And as always – to my muse – Lynton Viñas

Catalogue Number: 8341-945-849

ISBN: 978-1-928183-24-2

Fireside Books – Victoria, British Columbia
Peninsula Publishing Consortium

Introduction

Intense Darkness All of a Sudden

Edgar Rice Burroughs once described how the moon shone down out of a cloudless sky on a man named Tarzan, making the large white orb seem so close to the earth that you could touch it. The moon was like that on this night when Lynton Viñas was making her way to the continent where the fictional Tarzan had lived.

The world renowned demon fighter was filled with excitement as she sat on the plane that was circling Cape Town, South Africa, getting ready to land. She reached over and took her beloved Wayne's hand, looked over at him and let that voluptuous smile slowly creep across her succulent, puffy lips that seemed to always be begging for a kiss, and the moon this night was exactly as Burroughs had described it in his book over 100 years ago. She was about to embark upon a great adventure at the International Hotel School, where she had been accepted to study advanced hotel management.

Lynton was tired and even bewildered with some melancholia from all her demon hunting adventures, had given up her singing career, and was now determined to move her life in a new direction at the ripe old age of 31. She had been the youngest graduate ever from the Cambridge School of Law in the Philippines, but at only 20, she found out in a hurry that the law was never applied equally to the rich and poor. The poor had to pay for transgressions behind bars of brutality, but the rich got a slap on the wrist and were sent on their way by a system that did not know the meaning of justice. One year as a public defender had convinced her that until society embraced a more equitable economic system there simply was no hope for those at the bottom of the economic ladder to receive even a modicum of justice.

Lynton's South African Adventure: Demon of Fire at the Karoo Escarpment

She tossed her law books into a chest, and embarked on a career singing and dancing in night clubs and malls in Macau, Hong Kong, Tokyo and Manila, but then she bought a cell phone and her life changed when she began hearing a voice that led her into a haunted house to battle demons. That was when she became renown for her demon fighting ability, but her most harrowing adventure dealing with ghosts that had designs on two children's souls in the notorious mansion on Balete Drive in Manila proved too much for her, and she determined to put her life on a more even keel and move in a completely different direction.

Her beloved Wayne, who was also the chronicler of her many adventures in the best selling books that had captured the imagination of readers in 51 countries and made her a household name, squeezed her hand and said, "This is the beginning of a great adventure darling, an adventure that will open up a whole new chapter in your life, and cause me a lot less worry. I am losing a subject for my books, but I am gaining a partner who will one day be General Manager of the Waldorf in New York City."

Lynton smiled broadly and replied, "More likely the manager of a Motel 6 in some tiny little town in the wilderness."

They laughed together as the plane eased onto the runway. Wayne looked out over the wing and saw a dark cloud slowly obscure the moon bit by bit. There was an intense darkness all of a sudden.

Prologue

Sparkled with Grandeur and Delight

The reality of the darkness that exists in the world is often difficult to fathom, because we all want to believe in the light, not the darkness. Lynton was in Cape Town in search of light. She had lived a life of deprivation as a child, caught like the vast majority of Filipinos in the depths of poverty as the nation that had once been the envy of Asia, spiralled ever downward as the country was turned over, like so many Third World nations, to corporations and the wealthy for exploitation. She had gone on the streets at 12 to hawk vegetables, sleeping in alleyways, so that her parents, who irresponsibly followed the dictates of the church to be fruitful and multiply, would have one less mouth to feed.

9

She tried to see that her siblings had enough to eat, but disease and a medical system based on greed, claimed four of them at an early age. Through tenacity and determination, she had clawed her way out of poverty, but the long, arduous climb had required 70 hour work weeks and a life devoid of most things people in more advanced countries take for granite. When she was offered a scholarship to study Casino and Hotel Management, she was reluctant at first as she assumed she was too old. However, her dear Wayne had lovingly told her that opportunity knows no age limit, and that she should put her life as a demon fighter aside, because it was costing her money rather than making her money. Most people she helped in fighting demons and ghosts were incapable of providing her with funds, and her dream of being a professional singer had lingered for years as she worked for peanuts in clubs all over Asia. It was time for her to finally do something for herself and prepare for the future.

She and Wayne zipped through customs, and climbed into a van for the trip to their hotel where they would stay temporarily while looking for an apartment. The gloom that had momentarily overcome Wayne had lifted as the cloud over the moon dissipated. This was the first visit to Cape Town for both of them, and they were immediately struck with the beauty of the place and also the cold. Winter in the southern hemisphere is from June until September, and they were both taken by surprise at the chilly weather. When one thinks of Africa, one generally thinks of hot, humid teeming jungles filled with exotic animals. This was not the case in Cape Town, as it was a vibrant city in which the people did not walk with lions, but rather, as the two would find out, walked with the quiet dignity of individuals who had put a dreadful past behind them and embraced forgiveness and harmony. There was a magic to the place, a feeling that a multi-racial, ethnically diverse populace could find common ground by embracing hope.

Lynton's South African Adventure:
Demon of Fire at the Karoo Escarpment

The fabulously beautiful Table Mountain to their right, as they peered out the side window of the van, dazzled and danced in the glistening moonlight full of loveliness and a kind of invitation to embrace this place as it seemed to wrap its arms around you and pull you into its magic. It was as if the magic of Cape Town was like a mother pulling a child into the arms of love and comfort. Still, within Wayne there was uneasiness, a brooding sense of intense weariness as if there was something lurking beneath the surface ready to cast a pall over the excitement they both felt.

What was behind those towering grey mountains? They were beckoning towers of solid rock that stood up against the dark sky to the north and kept the valley snug and safe, but it was as if there was something dark and brooding, unfriendly and dangerous lurking behind them, something that waited with anticipation; yes, waited in anticipation in the darkness. A feeling of dread gripped Wayne, but he fought back the urge to share it with Lynton, because he did not want to dampen her excitement.

The van pulled up in front of the Adderley Hotel and they walked into the vibrancy of Cape Town. Far to the west, the moon was casting its glow on the proud mountains of the dear old city.

There was a large stone church by the park in the distance from whence there streamed forth the stillness and pure radiance that appeared as a beacon to the storm-tossed heart of man. Neither Wayne, nor Lynton were religious, as they saw religion as just another method of control used to keep the poor pacified by the belief they would get their riches in the hereafter, but they both looked at each other and their eyes twinkled with recognition that there was something magical about this place.

Every fallen human being has disordered desires and attachments. We love what we shouldn't love, or we love what we should but often in a wrong way. We seek our own comfort, our own pleasure, our own will. We value what we want more than we value what is best for us. We do wrong, even if only in our hearts. These two people understood the debased nature of far too many who embraced greed, but they also sensed the hope of those who always seemed to be on the outside looking in. They were not saints, but they had genuine soft spots in their hearts for those on the margins of society. These were two people who reached out with compassion, not from fear that God would damn them into the eternal fires of a hell, in which they did not believe, but because they had good hearts. Above all they understood the dark night of the soul, and how men used fear to control people. Fear was what kept people in line, made them not rock the boat or question the order of things.

They picked up their bags, and entered the hotel, where bright, smiling faces greeted them and extended the true hand of hospitality. They walked into their luxuriously appointed room, stood by the window, and looked out at a city that glistened and sparkled with grandeur and delight.

Chapter 1

The Heart is a Lonely Hunter

Edgar Rice Burroughs was long dead, and the character he created, Tarzan, was assumed to be fictional, but truth is often stranger than fiction, because Tarzan was real and he had asked Burroughs, whom he met while Burroughs was on safari in 1910, to be sure his character was fictionalized, because he wanted no part of fame or what he considered inglorious notoriety. The real Tarzan was a man called Barbizon and like Burroughs was long dead, but his son, his grandson and now his great grandson had lived in the jungles of Africa to embrace a life free of what was called civilization.

These were men who went to Cambridge and Oxford, but when they were exposed to what was called civilization; they were repulsed by the greed that ruled the world in complete disregard for economic justice, and they ultimately returned to more equitability and peacefulness in the jungle.

The original Barbizon's wife, Jill, had died when she was only 37, and her son went to Oxford because his dad had promised to see he was educated. After university, he lived in London until he was 32, but as his father aged, the son started worrying about him and returned to be by his side. They lived in relative obscurity for almost 25 years in the coastal jungle regions of Angola, but each passing year civilization crept in on them and they moved further and further into the jungle. The original Barbizon's death was traumatic for his son. When he placed the body on the funeral pyre, he was 50 years old, and assumed that the line would end with him as he had never taken a wife, but while the body was burning, a native girl standing there with the tribe that had come to love Barbizon, too, reached down and whispered to the crying new Barbizon, "You are now the Lord of the Jungle, and you need a wife by your side. I am young, but I am wise and will make you a fine mate."

Remarkably, they had but one child, a boy. They named him Little Barbizon, and he grew into a remarkable man, who by the age of 14 was taller and more muscular than his father. He was schooled at home. He was admitted to Cambridge at 15, but he was no longer 100% white as his bloodline was now half-black, and there was much prejudice he had to endure while at Cambridge, and once he graduated, he made his way back to the Angolan jungle and found that his father had died. The natives hailed him Lord of the Jungle and he became the new Barbizon. He lovingly cared for his mother. However, a civil war raged in Angola, with South Africa fighting to help preserve Portuguese colonialism. They were serving as a proxy for the USA, which, as always, feared a communist takeover that might freeze out corporations and the wealthy from control. It was then that Barbizon's grandson led his people out of Angola into an isolated area of South Africa, known as Hanton Karoo, which was so isolated at the time, it was not even mapped.

Strewn with out-of-the-way villages called Nieuwoudtville, Hanover, Williston and very tiny Brandvlei, most of the country is still out of cell-phone reach today. The silence and star-smattered night skies restored Barbizon's faith in humanity. It was there that he met a white woman named Cecile, who was on a trek for the Smithsonian Institution to map the area. When her party entered the Karoo, he brazenly forbade them to climb the sacred Karoo Escarpment which protected the natives from the onslaught of civilization. The topography of eastern South Africa is dominated by dramatic transitions. Along the coast, the individual mountain ranges of the Cape Fold Belt are interrupted by wide valleys that run from east to west. Beyond the northernmost of these ranges, the elevation drops off dramatically into an expansive basin called the

Lynton's South African Adventure: Demon of Fire at the Karoo Escarpment

Eastern Cape Karoo. Encircling the northern margin of the basin is the continent-spanning cliffs of South Africa's Great Escarpment. To this place, Cecile took an instant liking that bordered on an obsession, as she saw it as an opportunity to restore balance to her life, as the time there slowed to the rhythm of sheep, wheat and lucerne farming in the shade of the Hantam Mountain (a Khoi word meaning mountain of the red bulbs). Little disturbs the continuity of wide, open space until the cacophony of colour that follows good rains in the form of the annual spring flowers.

She and Barbizon fell in love, and this led to the birth of Barbizon the Fourth, whose mother died as he was being born. Barbizon never recovered from this loss of his wife and became a recluse, moving far back into the Karoo where he reared his son and taught him the ways of survival in a magical land that seemed lost in time. As time passed, Barbizon became ever more depressed until when his son was 18, Barbizon wondered off into the wilds one day and simply never returned.

Again, out of a cloudless sky the moon shone brightly as Barbizon moved further back into the desert ever further away from humanity. It was night, and Barbizon was abroad in the desert, the descendant of the original ape-man; mighty fighter, mighty hunter. Why he swaggered through the dark shadows of the sombre scrub forest he could not have told you. It was not that he was hungry; he had fed well this day. Perhaps it was the very joy of living that urged him from his normal abode further back into the scrub where the preying eyes of civilization might be blinded, and he could escape from the realities of a world his father had taught him to hate. Still, his father, Cambridge educated, had instilled a love of learning in his son, a sense that knowledge was power.

The desert of the moon was much different than the desert of the sun. There was darkness yes, but in that darkness was a primal light that guided Barbizon ever forward toward the moon with its eerie light dancing in the distance. The roar of nocturnal beasts, the dark of the desert night are as different as one might imagine the lights and shades of another world to differ from those of our world; its beasts, its blooms, and its birds are not those of the sun – the day. It was because of these differences Barbizon loved to investigate the desert by night. Not only was the life another life; but it was richer in numbers and in romance; it was richer in dangers, too, and to Barbizon danger was the spice of life. And the noises of the desert night - the baying of the wild donkey, the scream of the leopard, the hideous laughter of the hyena, were music to the ears of a man in perfect harmony with his surroundings.

The soft padding of unseen feet, the rustling of sparse leaves and browned grasses to the passage of majestically fierce beasts, the dancing sheen of preying eyes flaming through the dark, the million sounds which proclaimed the teeming life that one might hear and scent, though seldom see, constituted the appeal of the nocturnal jungle to Barbizon.

On this night, he had swung a wide circle toward the east first and then toward the south, and now he was rounding back again into the north. His eyes, his ears and his keen nostrils were ever on the alert. Mingled with the sounds he knew, there were strange sounds which he never heard except after the warmth of the day had passed into the chill of the night. He always heard them below the far edge of the big water-sounds emanating from the raging river near his lair. These sounds often caused Barbizon profound speculation. They baffled him because he thought that he knew his jungle so well that there could be nothing within it unfamiliar to him. Sometimes he thought that as colours and forms appeared to differ by night from their familiar daylight aspects, so sounds altered with the passage of day and the coming of night, and these thoughts roused within his brain a vague conjecture that perhaps something was strangely amiss in his world, the world of the Karoo. He had never accepted the superstitions of the Karoo, as he was too well-read for that, but he was familiar with the supernatural, and being an intelligent man, with scores of books back in his tree house home, he was naturally fascinated by a famous Filipino demon fighter.

Having seen Lynton's picture on the back of the books, he had, as a virile young man, imagined what it would be like to touch her soft flesh, maybe even steal a kiss. He saw in her picture the illumination of a certain magic, a special quality that so many saw, a light that twinkled in her eyes and shone with the intensity of an angel.

Still, on this night, he was aware of something incredibly sinister about, something lurking, waiting stealthily in the deep darkness. The sun ruled the day, and the moon ruled the night, but there was something about this night that seemed to compete with the moon, seemed to want to blot out the bright light and bathe everything in eternal darkness. Thus functioned the somewhat untrained in modern ways man-mind groping through the dark night of ignorance for an explanation of the things he could not touch or smell or hear and of the great, unknown powers of nature which he could not see.

The scent of men suddenly penetrated his nostrils, mixed with the acrid odour of wood smoke. As Barbizon swung north again, wide to his left the scent was borne down to him upon the gentle night wind. Presently, the ruddy sheen of a great fire filtered upward through the foliage toward him, and when Barbizon came to a halt in the stubby trees near it, he saw a party of half a dozen black men huddled close to the blaze. They were dressed in black and had AK-47's slung over their shoulders. Americans would say they were hunters. I mean every hunter needs to fire ten rounds a second. Barbizon knew better, because these kinds of guns were not for hunting wild animals. Well, maybe they were, if you considered men wild animals. They were not in this isolated bit of Karoo to hunt big game. They had more nefarious intentions.

Back at the hotel, Lynton and Wayne settled in, and talked about what they would do for the next two weeks while they waited for school to start. They had a long conversation with the manager, Cassius, and he encouraged them to try something off the beaten path, something that most tourists neglected – the magnificent Karoo Escarpment.

It was this suggestion that put them on a direct course toward Barbizon's home. The same night Barbizon hunched in the scrub trees looking at the six black men with AK-47's, Lynton and Wayne were in a nearby camp waiting to head up the Karoo Escarpment. As mentioned previously, this was an area where cell phone service is almost non-existent even today, so the two of them were shocked when a Range Rover came roaring into camp with grand news for Wayne. One of his books had just been picked up for option to a movie company. He had to meet with the producer right away to firm up the deal. Lynton wanted to go back to Cape Town, but Wayne insisted she continue the trek and enjoy the scenery and he would be back in a week to ten days. She reluctantly agreed and watched forlornly as

Lynton's South African Adventure:
Demon of Fire at the Karoo Escarpment

Wayne headed back toward Cape Town seven hours away, where he caught a plane to Los Angeles, leaving behind Lynton who was about to have an encounter with the most unusual of characters – the Lord of the Karoo, Barbizon.

Barbizon wondered what the men were doing in the Karoo, but his interest was also piqued by the sound that his acute hearing picked up far away near the escarpment. He heard the sound of a motor. Was someone else on their way over the escarpment? If so, he wanted to warn them off, because he had sworn to protect the Karoo people from the incursion of so-called civilization. They had lived for so many years able to avoid the modern world, and they wanted no part of it as their chief, Mantulu, had lived in the city, along with his two sons and wife, and he knew that so-called civilization held nothing his tribe needed. They lived in a paradise free of want and above all free of material things. Theirs was a utopia of sorts, as they had not been infected with the evil of greed.

Lynton's South African Adventure:
Demon of Fire at the Karoo Escarpment

This was no ordinary party of hunters, as while Barbizon's ears picked up the far away purr of a motor no one else heard, his eyes picked up a sight that generally meant trouble – a white man who meandered out of a tent, and was obviously in charge as all the natives there got quiet.

He pointed down at the fire where coffee was brewing and one of the men, like a dutiful slave, bowed and scrapped in supplication, serving him as if he were some ancient king in an ancient land. Now, it is not my intention here to paint all whites with a broad stroke of condemnation, but in Barbizon's experience they usually brought with them an insidious disease that spread like an epidemic ensnaring all in its evil. The disease was one for which it appeared there never was and never would be a cure. It is a disease that has plagued mankind since the beginning of time – greed. Barbizon had never left the Karoo, had never lived anywhere near a city, but he had heard his father talk of the evils that seemed to predominate there and trap people in poverty and despair, because the few got more and more while the poor were made to toil in obscurity for minuscule wages so those at the top could enjoy lives of luxurious splendour that were built on the backs of cheap labour. This was the way of the outside world that knows no compassion.

Those in the outside world would categorize the Karoo as backward and primitive. Theirs was a society with no economic surplus, but all in the tribe shared their land, resources, products and labour. There was a great capacity within them all for love and solidarity, because no one was in competition, and all knew that if they were needy, others would extend the hand of compassion. Americans called this socialism or even worse, communism. Americans had a system that blamed the poor for being poor and always let the good things flow to those at the top where lavish welfare was provided through tax breaks and preferential treatment, while the poor were ignored, or if they were lucky, had a bone tossed them from the table of plenty where the rich dined.

Lynton's South African Adventure:
Demon of Fire at the Karoo Escarpment

The white man Barbizon saw he instantly recognized as an American when he heard him speak. There was a tinge of intense intelligence to his tone as he bade the six blacks goodnight and went back into his tent.

Barbizon thought deep and long about what his father had taught him in regards to mankind's eternal pursuit of personal wealth while ignoring a higher calling to show compassion for the masses.

His father had told him that there is great human capacity for love and sharing, but the capacity for aggression and cruelty shows up when there is some economic surplus, but not enough for the whole tribe or nation to share the wealth. This is class society, the beginning of so-called civilization. In this caldron of inequity are class domination, severe cruelty and greed by those at the top who want to control those at the bottom. Throw into this religion as a tool for the wealthy to convince the poor that their reward will be in heaven where the streets are paved with gold and the last shall be first and the first shall be last, and you have a populace that is easily manipulated to serve the rich. Barbizon's father had seen through the charade of capitalism and thoroughly rejected it and returned to the escarpment area where his beloved Karoo people were all equal and where greed was effectively kept at bay. His father had sold the family estate in England and donated all funds to a group of charities and retuned to paradise.

As his father used to say, "The class war has been raging for eternity, but it is finally over, and the rich won. The struggle for justice and freedom has been sacrificed at the altar of greed."

His father often said, "In our beloved Karoo Land there is no class antagonism, because the free development of each is the condition for the free development of all." He deeply revered his father and missed him so much. He assumed his father's grief, after all those years, had just become too much for him and he decided that the pain could only end with his death. He left a simple note for his son – "I go to meet my destiny.

You must meet yours too my son. Good luck and I love you."

Then, he looked at one of the black men and knew why they were there. It was not for the gold that lay on the valley floor. That was a prize many had sought but failed in the pursuit of that which meant nothing to those who called this valley home. The people of this land were peaceful, but those from the outside world who came to exploit the riches there were dispatched with great swiftness by the normally peaceful people. They always fiercely defended their home from the incursions of those driven by greed.

Yet, Barbizon knew this was much worse than greed. The symbol on the man's chest was an evil omen.

Symbol on the Man's Chest

These were not ordinary men, and they were in pursuit of that which his father had warned him of so often. Yes, these were members of the Cult of Kalma, an ancient organization of those who worshiped the devil, and Barbizon was up to doing battle against any beast, but the beast these men were in search of was fiercer than any he had ever encountered. The beloved Karoo people rarely ventured into the Valley of the Wind where the devil was rumoured to abide in the darkness of the Baldasack Caves, and that was the symbol Barbizon saw on the man's chest, the symbol of Kalma, the name given the Lord of the Underworld. None of the Barbizon's had ever dared cross into that valley and enter the caves, because there was simply no need to tempt fate, but these men were here for evil. Barbizon sensed it.

Fate is a determined hunter, and fate had found Barbizon, though he did not realize it. He felt a cold chill run up and down his spine. This was a man who had no fear, but the thing on this person's chest had been something his father had warned him was a symbol of those who bowed in supplication to the devil. None of the Barbizon's believed in heaven, but they had all believed in hell, the kind of man-made hell that trapped people in the circle of evil that one man could impose on another. The outside world was filled with the evil of those who hoarded all the wealth and accumulated more and more on the backs of the poor who were nothing but grease in the giant machinery of capitalism that ground up people and destroyed them in the name of profit.

Brown branches, brown branches,
I see you beckon; I follow!
Evil is the place you guard,
there in the hot steamy hollow.
Wherein he lies in the darkness,
under the thorns of evil flowers,
heedless at last, in the silence,
of these wailing midsummer hours.

But in slumber, it may be, the lord

Lynton's South African Adventure: Demon of Fire at the Karoo Escarpment

of darkness is plotting evil now,

and the evil shines about his brow,

As he dwells in the dark place deep in the hollow

wherein he dreams of those who follow.

Green wind from the green-gold branches,

what is the song of death he brings,

and of demonic evil he lovingly sings?

Evil is there in the bow,

for any with keen eyes to see.

Can you sense something foul?

What are all the songs for you and me?

Deep in our hearts of forgotten summer,

the wind, the birds, the beasts are still,

but the heart is a lonely hunter

that hunts on a lonely hill.

Black is that hill and set far in a shadowy place;

the darkness within has an evil face:

the evil one shoots arrows of nasty breath,

with the horrible stench of death.

Humanity moans of a sorrow olden,

as lost to evil is something golden.

The cold wind of evil swirls in the hollow,

As the evil one whispers, "come and follow."

O never a green leaf whispers,

where the green-gold branches swing:

O never a song you hear now,

where one was wont to sing.

Here in the heart of summer,

evil will not be so still,

the heart is a lonely hunter

and hunts on a lonely hill.

Baldasack Caves Entrance

(Where the Karoo rarely ventured)

Chapter 3

The Darkness of Evil

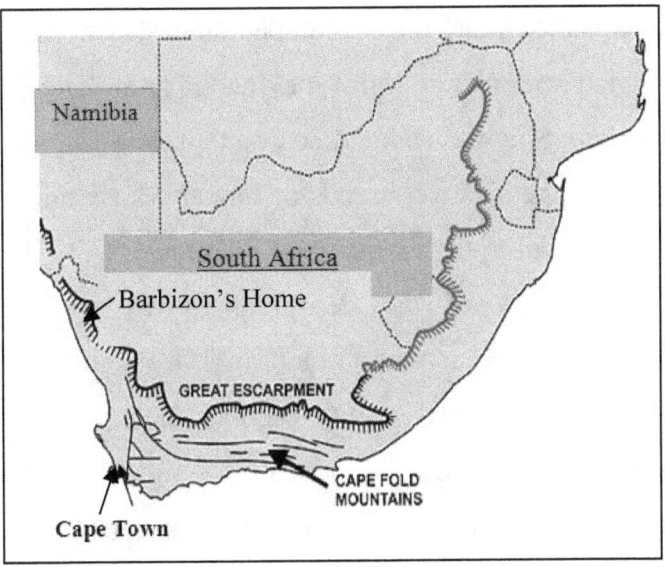

Thinking of his beloved father had brought tears to Barbizon's eyes. He turned and decided to go back toward the escarpment and see what was going on there. He had two problems now, and he feared he would have to decide which the greater threat was, but little did he know he was about to meet the dynamic dynamo!

Time is the tapestry which is life. It is eternal, constant, unchanging. It is gathered together from the portals of pleasure and misery to weave a design that is never finished. A thread from here, a thread from there, another from out of the past that has waited years for the companion thread without which the picture must be incomplete. Fate is patient. She waits a hundred or a thousand years to bring together two strands of thread whose union is essential to the fabrication of her tapestry, to the composition of the design that was without beginning and is without end. In 1989 a cult was born in the desert of Karoo, as a strange occurrence raised the demon devil from the bowels of the earth to spread evil at a future time.

In recent times, into the caves of the Baldasack came a man named Agus, who was inclined toward fanaticism. In today's world, the fanatical Muslim is branded by the fanatical Christian, who tries to impose his or her will on people through the elimination of secularism, a fanatic. One fanatic calling another a fanatic is the way of the modern world. The man or woman who worships money is a fanatic. The person who is obsessed with sex is a fanatic. The person who cannot control the desire to drink is called an addict, but is he or she not a fanatic of drink? Labels are easy to place, but more difficult to explain. The Palestinian who hungers for food or thirsts for water while Israel cuts off the supplies grabs a bomb and blows himself and others up. He is a fanatic, but what of the ones who created the condition in the first place? Are those people not fanatics also? 9/11/2001 was the act of fanatics, but what of the American fanaticism that stirred the cauldron of discontent that led to the cries of "Allah Akbar," as the planes ploughed into the twin towers? American government propaganda is used to make patriotic robo-tons dutifully recite the Pledge of Allegiance, put their hands over their hearts or salute the flag. Is this not breeding patriotic fanatics as Hitler did in Germany during his initial rise to power, as he wanted to prepare the youth to die for the fatherland? Fanatics take many forms, not all evil, but far too many hug the dark side, embracing man's inhumanity.

Such was Agus, who fled the evil of apartheid (separation of the races) in Cape Town and came into the desert in 1980 as a 25 year old with a 15 year old child bride whom he had bought from a father and mother left destitute by an evil system called capitalism that aggrandized greed. In Apartheid Era South Africa, this system of greed depended on the slave-like labour of blacks to serve the interests of the white minority.

It was into this system Agus was born and the system bred hatred in him, a hatred that drove him away from a church that seemed to simply acquiesce to the inequity of racism that kept the blacks in servitude and also kept blacks and whites alike as economic slaves to the moneyed class.

His sense of persecution was justified, but he let the evils of apartheid turn his heart evil, too. George Bush's attempt in the early 2000's to fight terrorism with terrorism only led to an increase in terrorism, not its elimination. Using evil to fight evil is the justification of a fool, but Agus was no fool, just a man who had led a life of injustice in an unjust system that was now gone, but he could not let the evil of the past go. Thus were sown the seeds of discontent that led him to embrace evil, and that evil was now about to manifest itself in the worst way imaginable.

On Agus' chest was the symbol of evil as embraced by the cult of Kalma, and beneath it were words that Agus now lived by.

Umbutu Kalma
Din Belini Swez

Translated as *"Hail Kalma by Hate Embraced"*

41

Lynton's South African Adventure:
Demon of Fire at the Karoo Escarpment

We shall move on as this story unfolds, but remember Agus for we shall return to him soon and see that evil is not an immediate manifestation but is like a slow simmering stew. Evil can simmer too, and it did in the heart of Agus, who was about to unleash the devil himself to satisfy his own desire for evil in a world he had grown to hate. Thus, fate sometimes does the dance of a thousand sorrows and those sorrows were about to embrace Barbizon and Lynton in the very near future, courtesy of what was in the caves.

The South African moon, still high in the sky, was hidden from the face of the earth by solid cloud banks that enveloped the loftier peaks of the mysterious, impenetrable vastnesses of the forbidding Karoo Escarpment that frowned perpetually upon the valleys, few known to man.

From far above this seeming solitude, out of the heart of the densely banked night mist, there came, swiftly striding through the brush, the mighty Barbizon. He looked off to his left, moving from tree to tree, toward the Baldasack Caves that were

always avoided by the Karoo, for within was
rumoured to be the Lord of the Underworld,
Kalma, the evil minion of despair who spit fire.
Barbizon's keen ears heard a faint rumbling sound
coming from the direction of the caves. At times it
grew in volume until it attained terrifying
proportions; and then gradually it diminished until
it was only a suggestion of a sound, only to grow
once again in volume and to again retreat. Still,
Barbizon had heard the roar of engines at the base
of the escarpment and he needed to see if, indeed,
some other outsiders were trying to penetrate the
veil of isolation that had kept the Karoo people
safe from civilization for so many years. The
sound was gone now, but he had to know if those
at the escarpment might have left someone behind.

Still, he could not get his mind off the
Baldasack Caves to his left as they had for so long
been almost invisible in the mysteriousness of fear
that they had for all who lived in the area. It was
the place of demons he had always been told, and
he saw no need to question the way of the Karoo,

for they were wise and just people. The caves were deep in the concealing vapours that hid them from the earth and hid the earth from them. This was Barbizon's world. He knew no other and did not want to know another.

Lynton stared up at the escarpment as she was maybe only 500 metres from the top. She knew that she must cross a lofty range of mountains to get to the other side, and Cassius had told her that the beauty was to be observed from the outer side, and that what lay behind the escarpment was dissolute country not worth the effort to see, and anyway, there were rumours of danger lurking there. Still, she felt compelled to venture forward despite the protestations of her guide that it was not wise to venture over the escarpment.

The guide and the three men accompanying him as assistants did not know Lynton and her propensity for adventure. Put a barrier before her and it was like waving a red cape before a bull. She would invariably charge full-steam ahead. She always got a kick out of what Wayne had said when she described herself as a bull charging for a red cape: "Lynton my darling, despite the fact that bulls are males, what most people don't know is that bulls are colour blind, and you are far too often blind to the danger that might lurk behind that cape."

Lynton had been indulging in considerable high powered thinking, intermingled with the regret that she had not gone back with Wayne, but she was there now, and she needed to see what was on the other side of the escarpment. She was a woman of keen intelligence, fully competent to understand that grave danger often waited in the darkness of a world that far too often embraced evil.

A few weeks before this night, in New York City, a dark, mysterious man was boarding the private jet of a billionaire who had instructed him to wing his way to Cape Town where a man named Agus would meet him, and take him to a place in the interior called the Karoo Escarpment, where all the riches of the world would be made available if he did just as instructed. Harry Smith was a slightly stoop shouldered, small, quiet, modest, scholarly looking middle aged man with horn rimmed spectacles, which he wore not because of any defect of eyesight but rather donned them in the belief that they added a certain dignity and mark of intelligence to his appearance. That his spectacles were fitted with plain glass was known only to himself and his optician. Graduated from university with a Ph.D. at twenty, he had a somewhat understandable arrogance about him as his intelligence was far superior to most. That is, of course, if intelligence is judged by degrees, not wisdom.

This was the white man Barbizon had seen in the camp. We may leave him now with Agus in the Karoo, with his sinister intentions in service to the corrupt of heart and soul billionaire who had spent his entire life in pursuit of more and more, because, though he had inherited billions from his father, he was never satisfied, because deep down, he felt inadequate when compared to his father.

Harry Smith was his ambassador of greed, his ambassador of evil.

Meanwhile, the ruler of Russia, a man who had honed his skills in the KGB, an organization akin to the USA's CIA, looked over at the young KGB agent, Eric Kabowski and said with determination, "Go into the Karoo, for now is the time when we can get what we have always sought. The glorification of the fatherland is at hand."

Kabowski bowed and backed out of the room. The evil ruler of Russia smiled at a girl there with him and said, "You imbecile of desire, come to daddy and let me love you for a long time, for I am invigorated with passion."

The young, nubile woman danced as Salome must have for Herod the Great when she demanded the head of John the Baptist, but this young woman would ask for nothing, for she knew the evil of the man whose arms she fell into offered nothing but tormented hell for those who did not obey him and cater to his desires. This was a man devoid of any humanity, a man who was, himself, every bit as evil as the billionaire, as well as Mr. Smith and whatever evil being lurked in the bowels of the Baldasack Caves.

Russia's leader knew of Barbizon and turning to his companion, whispered softly, "There was an ape-man in the Karoo who helped the people there keep us from what we need to finally bring the world to its knees and make Russia the great nation it once was. We will be great again."

Giggling, the now naked girl, said, "And is not this ape-like man still there?"

"His weakling son has tried to take his place. The father disappeared into the wilds, and, no doubt, has been killed by the wild creatures that still roam freely there. Come now my lovely and let this wild creature devour you."

While the two were frolicking in desire, Kabowski was already winging his way to South Africa and as he changed planes in Addis Ababa, Ethiopia, fate took a seat beside him in the form of Harry Smith. Now, the plan was in full motion as the two representatives of demented men were in unison committed to the plan that would conjure foul evil in the Karoo.

Fate is like a starlit night. Any star upon which you gaze may suddenly burn out and start its plunge into oblivion. As Barbizon stood at the top of the escarpment looking down on Lynton and her four companions, he heard from behind the faint sound of feet scurrying toward him. He turned and waited patiently, instinctively knowing as the sound of the feet upon the moist earth got closer and closer, that it was Chief Mantulu.

Barbizon's uncanny ability to catalogue the very sounds of people's feet had been taught him by his father. On this night, he leaned onto a tree and sighed as his sinewy, lithe, muscular body seemed to pulsate with a premonition of coming evil, but Mantulu could not be the bearer of evil, thought Barbizon, for he was a man of compassion who had gone to America as a youth to live in the jungles of concrete and steel. He had found it wanting and returned to his people to embrace hope in a home that was a paradise of love and compassion. However, he could be the bearer of bad news, and that bothered Barbizon.

He greeted Mantulu with a smile as he walked through the clearing toward him. "My friend, I hope you do not bear bad news."

"I am afraid we have problems Barbizon. For long we lived at peace with all men," explained Mantulu; "we did not make war upon our neighbours. We wished only to plant and harvest in security. But there has come into the Karoo six blacks and two whites whom we know are here for some ill deed."

Barbizon thought intently about the party he had seen. It was his assumption there was only one white man among them, but perhaps there were two. Maybe the other white man had stayed in the tent.

Barbizon said, "I have seen them. They are camped at the Umbari Fork in the Great Brak River. Keep an eye on them my friend, and together we will see that they do not defile our homeland. Be weary though, for they are not here for the normal treasures most seek. They are here for more nefarious intentions. They are here to try and commune with the Lord of the Underworld Kalma, whom we have been taught to fear."

Mantulu got a concerned look and said, "Are we to kill them?"

"Only if we must, my friend. I am going to check on another party that is at the base of the escarpment. Go back to your village and be patient. I shall be there shortly and we will decide what must be done."

Again, fate was about to rear its head, as the two bade farewell to one another and Barbizon moved ever closer to the edge of the escarpment and looked down. About 300 metres below he saw a camp with a few guides and then he observed a remarkably beautiful woman walk out from a tent.

I have described Lynton Viñas in many books, but one more time is necessary as she is older and has ripened like a flower opening to the warm noon-day sun. It seems that, as with many women, maturity made her like fine wine fermented to complete perfection. She had mellowed with age and there was a refinement to her beauty that reminds one of Oscar Wilde in his descriptive splendorous pleas that women were to be sipped deliberately, savoured and gradually devoured with passion.

Lynton was a woman of infinite charm, but one needed to tread lightly with her. So delicate was she that she might well hear daisies grow. Her silken black hair cascaded like a gentle waterfall over her dainty shoulders. She was a bright angel twinkling with delight. You knew that nothing could ever tarnish her goodness. Like lily white snow, she was light and delicate, but you knew that within beat a heart of determination.

She had a sculpted full figure for a small woman who was not anorexic but voluminously alluring. The calves on her legs were muscular from years of dancing and playing volley ball. Her waist was tapered but there was just an ever so slight pouch to her stomach that jiggled slightly as she walked with long confident strides. She had a gleaming complexion and a pair of arched eyebrows looked down on sweeping eyelashes. Her delicate puffy high cheekbones framed a flat, Asian button nose. A set of dazzling, angel-white teeth gleamed with a sparkling light and her puffy, full, ripe lips seemed to always be begging for a kiss. Her enticing, constellation-dark eyes gazed up at the escarpment where Barbizon was crouched in wonderment that someone so beautiful had come to his beloved Karoo. He immediately recognized her with his keen night vision. This was the woman he had read about in the books that had immortalized the dynamic dynamo. This was the demon hunter, Lynton Viñas. Yes, he was about to join forces with the dynamic dynamo!

This woman had so sweetly grown. Her gentle, soft, perky breasts rose and fell with rhythmic precision as she breathed the crisp air near the top of the escarpment.

Barbizon gazed down upon her, and felt the rise of passion that he had experienced so often but had never shared with any woman. He squinted his eyes and beheld the beauty of the ages, the Taj Mahal of titillation was walking about the camp. Each sway of her provocative hips sent chills through Barbizon as he stared in total concentration at her, thinking how it would be best to approach the party below so that he might converse with Lynton and ask for help.

Fate had brought her, thought Barbizon, to the edge of the escarpment so that he could use her skill and knowledge of demons to fight against the evil of those who had come to the Karoo, for he knew that the party back near the Baldasack Caves was there to resurrect the demonic presence that was in the cave, waiting to unleash evil on the world.

As Barbizon prepared to enter the camp and demand all leave except Lynton, back near the Baldasack Caves, Agus, along with his two white companions, Harry Smith and Eric Kabowski, stood at the foot of the towering cliff that is the wall of the mighty crater of a long extinct volcano.

The entrance to the Baldasack Caves was so foreboding that no Karoo had dared enter them out of fear. The entrance resembled a skull and what lurked in the dank darkness of the caves was something that had been waiting for years to be released so that it could wreck havoc and terror on mankind.

One and all, they stood with faces raised toward the caves maybe 100 metres above. Upon each their countenance reflected the particular emotion that the occasion evoked - wonder, questioning, fear, and always rapt, tense listening, for from within the central cave, an ominous droning sound, the like of which not one of them had ever heard before, permeated the darkness that was engulfing them now. The sound grew in volume until it seemed to hover just above them, filling all the heavens with its terrifying threat; and then it diminished gradually until it was only a suggestion of a sound that might have been no more than a persistent memory rumbling in their heads; and when they thought that it had gone it grew again in volume until once more it thundered down upon them where they stood in awe.

Suddenly, the terrifying sound, swollen to hideous proportions, swept downward from the central cave opening toward them. It seemed to stop above them and vibrate for a moment and then a voice could be heard speaking first in English, then repeating the words in Russian. "Come forth into the liar of Kalma and bow before the exalted one." Then, at the entrance of the cave, stood a strange looking, apparition like figure - a terrifying thing - a great, dark, slimy abomination, which stared at them with piercing eyes.

Agus dropped to his knees, raising his hands in supplication toward the hideous thing. Harry and Eric stood erect, showing no emotion.

All began to move up the hillside toward the entity, as it backed into the cave. The porters had stayed back at camp, only Eric, Harry and Agus were moving toward the cave.

They entered into the cave timidly as the entity slowly moved backward. The thing now began to take on more solid form. Gaunt, in a space-like suit to the point of emaciation, its light white skin was pulled tautly over its bones. The bones pushed out against its skin, its complexion the ash gray of death, and its eyes pushed back deep into their sockets. It looked like a gaunt skeleton recently disinterred from the grave. What lips it had were thin and puffy. Removing its helmet, the now human-like entity gave off a strange and eerie odour of death and corruption. This was evil. This was evil personified.

Fall before this abomination
You weak and miserable creatures.
Here you are to seek glory,
And of this be especially sure,
To do aught good never.
Do ill as your sole delight,
As it is evil's damning will
Whose catastrophes the earth will chill.

That bold blight of catatonic confusion which blasphemes and bubbles at the centre of all evil - the boundless, bone-chilling demon of dank darkness, the Lord of the Underworld, whose name no lips could utter without fear, and who gnaws hungrily in inconceivable, unlighted chambers beyond all time amidst the muffled, maddening beating of vile moans of evil and the thin, monotonous whine of accursed souls; to which detestable beings dance in decadent delight to gloriously praise the evil they embrace, is the very core of despicable, blind, soul-damning love for the demonic. Yet, those there, save Agus, were there for the worst demon of all – greed.

The two foreigners were ready now to embrace an evil like no other the world had ever seen. Yet, their belief in Kalma was about playing a game of power, not a truly referential respect for the supposed Lord of the Underworld. This was not Kalma but a real man who displayed an outward appearance of despicableness, so none there, not even Agus truly believed in the preposterousness of a demon. Yet, they were willing to accept this manifestation, because, although they deemed it some type of magic trick, Kalma had the keys to unlock the Armageddon they were all in search of in that cave. Yes, the Cult of Kalma would be used by Harry Smith to further enrich his boss billionaire who was in cahoots with Russia's leader to make the entire world tremble before their evil. With Eric Kabowski, representing the President of Russia and by his side the loyal servant Agus, the Karoo area was about to understand the true meaning of evil. It was all about money to Harry's boss, but for Russia's President, it was about the raw power that would make him the most feared man in the world.

However, Agus was more than just Eric and Harry's guide. He was there to serve Kalma in a different way. He truly believed that revenge was a dish best served cold with the icy chill of indignation, but he would bow before this demon from hell so that his cold heart could be heated with the fires of hell to rain terror down upon those he saw as oppressors who had gone unpunished. As a child, he had suffered the horrid inequities perpetrated by the cruelty of apartheid.

He watched as his father and mother laboured for a wealthy white family, and never once were they shown respect by those for whom they toiled. Each day they had to leave the squalid slums outside the city to journey nearly two hours to a job that required 10 hours of back breaking labour. Then a two hour journey home to an unheated one room tin shack with no running water. This was the ugliness of racism that had been sanctioned by a government that used the Bible to actually justify separation of the races as the natural order of things as ordained by God.

The great, iconic humanitarian who led South Africa out of darkness, Nelson Mandela, had embraced forgiveness, even accepting the forgiveness of murder for those who repented and admitted their crimes. Agus was simply not willing to accept that the years of oppression could be washed away into a sea of tranquility. He wanted retribution, especially from the family for whom his parents laboured for so long, the very family that had abandoned them both when it was discovered they had joined a protest demanding the release of Mandela from prison. The two of them were fired and given no severance pay. For 30 years they had slaved for that arrogant family and then were cast aside with no compassion. He would ask a favour of Kalma, even if he had to give up his soul. All he desired was for that family to know pain and agony, the physical suffering that would cause them to plead for mercy. He wanted to watch them writhe in despair as the fires of hell consumed them. Oh, and he had a list of whites he wanted to pay for crimes that were forgiven by those more compassionate then he.

Thus the three men stood before what they assumed was Kalma, and prepared to embrace any abomination, any despicable act of depravity in order to achieve their sordid ends. But then the man removed his helmet and it was not Kalma, it was just an ordinary man in a sterile suit.

Meanwhile, Barbizon edged his way down the escarpment and walked brazenly into the encampment, where all stared in disbelief, and beside Lynton stood Thatoo Molmackmand, her guide. He whispered to Lynton, "It is the one they now call the new Lord of the Karoo. He is Barbizon."

Barbizon was a mere 26 years old, stood 6 feet 5 inches in height with the body of Adonis. As he slowly and methodically ambled through the encampment, all eyes were glued to him as his stride was cock-sure and his demeanour let everyone know this was not a man you messed with. He seemed to have a glow about him as you could sense that stars could form a constellation in his mesmerizing image. His face was so precisely chiselled that the heavens appeared to decree his physical perfection as a man.

Lynton stood in complete awe of what appeared to be the most perfectly sculpted man she had ever laid eyes on. She, who seemed to never be at a loss for words, stood in complete silence as he came to a halt no more than 5 feet from her. The ever talkative Thatoo stood there staring at him, trying to find words, when he finally managed to mumble, "You are Barbizon, Lord of the Karoo."

"I am he, indeed," he said without looking at Thatoo, keeping his dark eyes glued on Lynton, staring into her exotic dark eyes as he directed his words toward Thatoo. "You have no business going to the other side of the escarpment. It is the land of the mighty Karoo people."

He then let out a slight smile as he directed the next words toward Lynton, "But you I need on the other side of the escarpment, for I know who you are."

Lynton was shocked that he would recognize her, and asked, "And just how do you know me? I am only recently arrived here in this beautiful country."

The smile got broader now. "You are the famous demon fighter. It is indeed propitious that you have come."

Shocked at how well-spoken he was, Lynton offered an observation. "You are incredibly articulate."

"And you are incredibly beautiful," offered Barbizon.

"I am pleased you find me attractive."

"Not attractive. I said beautiful. You, I am sure, know there is delineation between the two."

"I stand corrected, but how may I ask do you know of me?"

"My father has an arrangement with the Looton Book Store in Cape Town. They send books on a regular basis here. Right here at the base of the escarpment, once a month, books are delivered and they are paid for with gold. I take the books back and my father and I always spend hours reading. I love the Lynton series. However, I never dreamed I would ever meet the dynamic dynamo."

"Well, I am very pleased to make your acquaintance."

Not in the form of a question, but as a direct command, Barbizon demanded in a strong voice, "You will come with me Ms. Viñas, as there is a demon that must be stilled."

Lynton, taken aback, looked over at Thatoo, then back at Barbizon. "I am not in the habit of being ordered to do something."

Barbizon lowered his head a bit, took a deep breath and sighed. "I apologize, it is just that I am about to face something with which I am not familiar. However, it is something that you have faced many times."

Smiling, Lynton said, "I accept your apology, and obviously, you are concerned about something in the supernatural realm. However, I am not here to deal with any demons. I have left that behind me."

Thatoo interjected, "She is here to study, and we are here in the Karoo to view the loveliness of this place with respect for the Karoo people's privacy, not chase some phantoms."

Barbizon looked directly at Lynton, his eyes almost hypnotic in the way he gazed into her eyes. "I know your commitment to justice and compassion. Would you turn your back on the Karoo people? Good and kind they are to all but those who would defile the valley on the other side of the escarpment. I can defeat any beast of the Karoo, even the worst beast of all, man. However, I have never come up against the supernatural, and like a miracle, here you appear, the world's most renowned demon fighter. I tell you that the Karoo people need your help. Please come with me, and help me protect them from this evil that is growing in the Valley of the Wind at the Baldasack Caves."

She looked over at Thatoo. He shook his head vehemently as he said, "No missy, absolutely not. This would not be wise."

Now, it has been often noted that telling Lynton Viñas no is a bit like telling a dog not to bark. She is a woman who enjoys a challenge and despite some trepidation she said, "O.K."

Thatoo shook his head in a stern manner as he pleaded with her. "Please, Dr. Frye will be upset with me. Please, please."

Smiling, Lynton said, "Do not worry about Wayne. I know how to handle him. Anyway, he has years of experience with me defying the norm. I think that is one reason why he is attracted to me."

Barbizon swept her into his muscular arms, lifting her with ease, turned and walked up the side of the escarpment as she said, "Please, I need some clothes, a tooth brush and some female things."

"I will get you what you need from the wilds of the Karoo. All things are provided by nature, if you know how to find them."

Looking at Barbizon's sinewy, muscular, body that glistened in the moonlight as he pranced boldly up the side of the escarpment carrying her, Lynton felt a slight surge of passion as this man, wearing only a small loin cloth of deer hide covering his lower extremities was the most incredibly physically imposing person she had ever seen.

She looked back over his shoulder at Thatoo and said, "Do not worry, and tell Wayne that I shall contact him as soon as possible." She then turned to Barbizon and staring into his eyes said, "I am perfectly capable of walking."

Barbizon replied, "I am sure you are, but you have short legs. This will be faster."

Lynton's simple and scant apparel consisted of a loose fitting pair of shorts appearing to be made of flimsy, delicate material that was about 7 or 8 centremetres above her gorgeously alluring knees. Her lose fitting top went to midriff and exposed her belly that was taunt, but not muscular. Her bosom was bra free as she had been sleeping. Her sneakers were pink and seemed a bit out of place in the Karoo. She felt secure and safe in his arms, but thought to herself that this youthful denizen of the Karoo must be ignorant of the ways of the outside world. Though articulate beyond her expectations, she assumed that he was not formally educated, but self taught. She found him fascinating to say the least.

Reaching the top of the escarpment, she pleaded one more time to be put down, as she assumed her tiny 162 centremetres (5:2), 50 kilos

(110 pounds) body was too heavy even for this brawny specimen of manhood. Again, he denied her request, saying he needed to make good time and she would be unable to keep up.

She could not deny that she was somewhat aroused by this strange person, despite their age difference. She sighed and thought of Wayne, who had never exhibited any traits of jealousy. On the other hand, she warned him that she was a jealous woman, and if she caught him in a compromising dalliance, he would pay dearly. She was not a woman with whom one should ever trifle.

Lynton was all woman and the natural inclination of many women is to be a bit in awe of a true specimen of physical manhood. She had been in awe of Wayne, because of his intellect, not his physicality. Theirs was a relationship predicated more on intellectual rather than physical attraction. However, she did feel a bit of a physical attraction to Barbizon to her chagrin.

As the swift-footed Barbizon moved gracefully and assuredly through the scrub, she took a deep breath, relaxed in his arms and fell into slumber, which was good, because she would get little rest in the future. What lay ahead was a taxing journey into the darkness of evil.

Chapter 3

Terror Waiting to be Unleashed

It was almost dawn when Lynton opened her eyes and turned slowly to look about in all directions. She saw precipitous cliffs completely hemming a small circular valley, near the center of which was a river.

Suddenly, a group of spear carrying warriors seemed to pop out from nowhere. They came slowly, timidly nearer her, obviously curious as to why Barbizon had brought her. He spoke to them in a language she did not understand, and Mantulu, as Barbizon lowered her from his arms, moved up to her and spoke in English. "You are welcome Lynton Viñas to our valley. Barbizon is sure you can help us. I hope that is true, because we fear great evil is afoot."

71

They all crouched down in a circle and Mantulu and Barbizon related to her the history of the caves and how it was assumed they harboured a demon of the foulest kind.

"I have seen many strange things," offered Lynton, "but I have never been thoroughly convinced of but one true demon – man. Men are capable of the foulest deeds, and most often those deeds of evil are motivated by greed and the lust for power."

Mantulu said, as he signalled for Abrem, one of the warriors to come forward, "This is Abrem, and he has been observing what is going on at the cave."

Abrem took a deep breath and spoke in excellent English. "I was spying on two white men and a black at the entrance to the cave. There was an apparition of sorts appeared before them and they did not tremble in fear, but seemed to embrace the thing, eventually moving into the cave with it. It is hard to describe, as it was more mist than anything else, but you sensed its evil."

"Was there anything else unusual that you noticed? Maybe something that stood out?"

Arem looked down at the ground, seemingly in deep thought. "There, there, yes, there was a strange sound that seemed out of place in the cave. It was, let me see now. It was like the whine of a horse."

Lynton looked alarmed. "And you only heard it. You did not see it?"

"I did not, no, but we all know that within those caves lives the Lord of the Underworld, the great demon, Kalma."

"But you are sure there was a whining that sounded like a horse?"

"I am."

"You may know him as Kalma, but the ancient name is Cimeries in demonology. He is the dark prince of Africa that rules over all spirits of the continent. It is said that Cimeries sometimes rides on a black horse. The black horse in the Apocalypse represents famine, hunger, and economic breakdown. You heard the horse for sure?"

"I did."

Suddenly the morning damp air was filled with a scream of fear and horror that brought all there to their feet. It came from the direction of the caves. Barbizon said, "It comes from the Baldasack." He took Lynton's hand, and pulled her along as he and the 30 warriors moved quickly in the direction of the scream.

As they scurried toward the caves, walking up the eastern side of the Karoo Escarpment, which was the most treacherous route, but was being used to avoid detection, was a man named Danny Dampier. He was an American from New Orleans, and had by his side an AK-47, which he had purchased from an arms dealer in Namibia. He was on a mission that would satisfy his life long ambition to be somebody. For years he had been the enforcer for a mob boss, and he had seen his boss accumulate vast sums of wealth. So Danny double-crossed his boss, went over to the other side, and was a party to an assassination attempt on his old boss.

Lynton's South African Adventure:
Demon of Fire at the Karoo Escarpment

Unfortunately for Danny, the assassination attempt was botched and one of the guys caught in the attempt had fingered him. Danny knew the power of his boss made him nothing more than a dead man walking, and he would not be walking for long. So, Danny very quietly slipped out of the country, and wound up on a tramp steamer headed for the Namibia coastal town of Oranjemund.

A young man came and sat down in the chair next to his. He looked over at Danny and smiled. "Good morning," he said. "Lovely weather we're having."

Danny ignored him, shrugged his shoulders and looked the other way. Larry Hanover smiled at him despite Danny's discourteous nature. Larry opened a book, settled himself more comfortably in his chair and started reading. Danny eventually got up and left.

The following morning when Danny came on deck he found that the young man had preceded him. Danny elected to be more courteous this time as he said, "Good morning."

The young man looked up from his book and said nothing. Danny was not offended, as he figured he deserved it. He nodded his head and said, "Must be an interesting book."

"It is," he said. "It is about a Filipino demon hunter."

"Interesting subject I suppose. Are you on a pleasure trip?

"Well, I hope it will be," replied Larry, "but it is largely what might be called a business trip, too. Scientific investigation, I am a scientist."

"Pay well does it?"

"Not very, but I get by."

Danny sighed and said, "I ain't never been outta America before. My first trip aboard this is."

"So, you have never been to the African continent before my friend. You will find it fascinating."

"Sure I will. Only thing I know about Africa is Tarzan movies."

"Then you are in for a really big surprise. You will find many of its cities with far more amenities than the USA, and actually many have less poverty."

"Well, can't imagine any place being better than the good old USA, but I wore my welcome out there. What country you from?"

"I am from Great Britain, London to be exact."

"O.K., we call that England where I come from. Same thing I guess."

"Not really I am afraid. England is part of the country of Great Britain, which is made up of Scotland, Wales, Northern Ireland and, of course, England."

"So," offered Danny, "where you going?"

"I am going on a safari to the Karoo Escarpment."

"Safari, uh?"

"Yes," replied Larry. "There will be some people assisting me."

"What say I go with you, mister? I don't understand your racket, but I won't demand no cut-in whatever it is. I got money and can pay my share."

Larry thought for a minute as he sized up Danny. Maybe he could be valuable in an emergency. Yet he hesitated. He knew nothing about the man. He might be a fugitive from justice. He might be anything. Then again, what he had in mind for him, being a fugitive might be a positive. He leaned forward and said, as he extended his hand, "You are in."

Smiling, Danny grabbed his hand and shouted, "Sounds good to me."

Now, eventually there was Lynton and Barbizon with the warriors, Eric Kabowski and Harry Smith, along with Danny Dampier and Larry Hannover concerned with the caves at Baldasack. All were being weaved methodically into that grand tapestry of fate.

One might wonder how Danny and Larry managed to get to the Karoo, so that is a story which requires some explanation, as they had crossed the Namibian border to the Karoo.

The two of them had landed at Oranjemund, but went immediately to an isolated ranch near the

Karoo where the safari of the two white men and seven black porters, with a guide, made their way slowly toward the mighty Karoo Escarpment. The trek continued into the barren area near the escarpment when Danny asked if there were any lions about.

"There is my friend," replied Larry. "They are only a few lions left in the wild, so they are rarely seen. However, this area is known to have a few here abouts."

Carrying the acquired AK-47 by his side, Danny felt no fear as he said, "That why you brought me along, because I am handy with a gun?"

"Perhaps being handy with a gun is indeed an attribute I appreciate, but it has nothing to do with lions. You know the most sinister beast about is man, and I am beginning to wonder if you have killed some men in your day."

"Maybe."

"How would you like to make an awful lot of money?"

Danny's ears perked up and his eyes bugged out. "Money is always good?"

"Then we may get you some, my friend. I am here to decipher the authenticity of something very important that, in the wrong hands, could destroy the world as we know it. I am here to seek out information that might well lead to a discovery that will actually shake the foundations of civilization."

"Well, for the right amount of money, I'd probably bump off my own mom."

"It will not come to that, but you might have to use that gun you are carrying."

"You don't have to go into details. I am committed to this project. Whatever it might be, you can count on me."

"That's good, because when the time comes, when I give you the signal, I want you to kill whomever I say."

Danny was a man who knew how to follow orders, and he could not believe his good luck at meeting Larry. "I'll do as I'm told – no problem."

Larry, as they trekked ever closer to the cave, said, "We are going to meet some people who are as evil as you could never imagine, and in their hands, is an evil of incredible power. In their hands, it is retribution for perceived wrongs of so many years that can be atoned for only with the spilling of blood. I shall spill their blood if necessary to prevent the spread of their evil that will kill many innocents."

"You can spill as much blood as you want as long as I get my money."

"You got it, Danny. It as good as in the bank."

Suddenly, aroused by a deafening scream, the two sprung to the alert, cocking their rifles, and their native guide, suddenly shouted, "Kalma, demon of Baldasack Cave, has claimed another victim. We go no further."

Larry, gun aimed at the head bearer, said, "You go or you die."

"We die either way. I agreed to take you only to the base of the escarpment, no further. We have done that and more. We go back now."

Larry stood stoically, looked over at Danny and said, "Let 'um go. We are almost there, anyway." He then reached in his shirt pocket and pulled out a worn piece of paper, unfolded it and continued, "This is the map to where we are going." He turned his back on the guide, and he and Danny walked up the side of the escarpment with determination.

Their ears perked up when they heard another terrifying scream. They moved cautiously forward and to their right appeared something that was shocking, causing them to blink their eyes in disbelief. They spotted, except for a loin cloth, a nearly naked white man bounding across the barren landscape with a woman in his arms, carrying her as if she were an infant. He was swift and sure, with a determined stride. Still, they both wondered where the scream was coming from, as it was obviously a woman in distress.

As they came into the clearing, there before them was a sight that chilled to the bone. In the top of a dead tree trunk was a beautiful woman, completely naked, and moving slowly toward her in a cautious manner was a huge jaguar. It was going to devour the tasty morsel, but, as all smart predators do, it was making sure there were no impediments to its intent to kill.

Temporarily mesmerized by the scene, Danny and Larry both stared for a second before raising their weapons simultaneously. They fired at the same time, and one, who knows which, missed while the other hit the jaguar in the lower left leg, the bullet, unfortunately, only wounding it slightly, and thereby, enraging it even more.

Aroused by the deafening noise of the weapon and enraged by the wound inflicted, bent upon swift and savage reprisal, the jaguar wheeled about and charged straight for Danny.

Danny was kneeling so as to take better aim for a second shot, while Larry took careful aim with his rifle. A great tree spread above the two men, a sanctuary they should have sought, but their minds were not upon flight, for, the enraged beast was giving them no time, as it bounded toward them with intensity. Danny again squeezed the trigger. The mechanism of the piece was set for a continuous discharge of bullets as long as Danny continued to squeeze. As the remainder of the one hundred rounds in the drum spurted forth; there was only a brief spurt of fire, and then the gun jammed. Larry tried to continue firing, but fear had suddenly overcome him and his aim was so bad that the bullets simply tore into the ground in front of the beast.

While all this was happening, Barbizon had placed Lynton on the ground, pulled his knife and was charging the jaguar. He hurled himself onto the jaguar's back and with a well-placed thrust drove the knife into its side.

Spellbound, Danny and Larry stood staring incredulously at the sight before them. They saw the giant jaguar turn quickly to seize his tormentor. They saw him leap and bound and throw himself to the ground in an effort to dislodge his opponent. They saw the free hand of the man repeatedly drive home the point of his knife in the tawny side of the raging jaguar. They were afraid to fire again out of fear they might strike the seemingly wild man who had mounted the beast.

From the tangled mass of man and lion there issued frightful snarls and growls, the most terrifying element of which came, not from the beast, but from Barbizon who was yelling with each plunge of his knife into the jaguar's flesh. The battle was brief, despite the remarkable tenacity of the animal. Finally, like all creatures that know their time has come, it let out one last mighty sigh and collapsed in a heap on the ground.

All the while, Lynton lay on the ground in awe of the man who had swept her into his strong arms and spirited her toward a rendezvous with whatever waited in the Baldasack Caves. As Barbizon stood over the mighty jaguar in triumph, she felt a surge of admiration for his primitiveness.

Barbizon, staring at Dampier and Hannover, motioned for Lynton to join him by the beast, which she willingly did without protest. The two of them walked toward Dampier and Hannover, as Barbizon motioned for the naked girl to climb down from her perch in the top of the dead tree trunk. Without any formalities or niceties, Barbizon demanded of Larry and Danny in a direct tone, "Who are you and what are you doing here in the Karoo."

Danny, not knowing how to respond simply looked over at Larry who, masking his real intent, said, "We are but two tourists on a journey of discovery. We simply have gone astray as our guides deserted us.

Barbizon was even more direct, as he had been taught to be straight-forward when conversing. He said with intensity "Tourists are not welcome in this part of the Karoo, and it is foolish for two people unfamiliar with the dangers of this land to be here without any guide. My guess is you are lying. Your intentions are more nefarious." He then motioned again for the naked girl to get down and she walked over and stood by his side.

Lynton's South African Adventure:
Demon of Fire at the Karoo Escarpment

Larry and Danny were taken aback by this seemingly wild man's articulations. It was then that Larry decided a more plausible explanation might be in order. "I am a scientist, a physicist to be more precise."

"A physicist, uh? That is someone, from what I have learned, who is concerned with the nature and properties of matter and energy. You are interested in the mechanics, heat, light, radiation, sound, electricity, magnetism, and the structure of atoms. What would a physicist find of interest in the Karoo?"

Lynton, standing by Barbizon's side was overwhelmed with the breadth of Barbizon's intelligence. Despite his lack of any formal schooling, his depth of knowledge bordered on the amazing. Meanwhile, Larry and Danny were stunned and awed by his cleverness. It was this respect for Barbizon's luminosity that motivated Larry to be a bit more honest. "I work for the Society of Atomic Scientists at Cambridge. It appears that some strange radiation has been detected here in the Karoo, specifically near the Caves of Baldasack. They have asked me to investigate. I apologize for being evasive before, but I prefer anonymity, as it makes conducting my research easier."

Larry and Danny instinctively gripped their weapons tighter as Mantulu and his warrior's showed up, but Barbizon, with a wave of his hand said, "Do not fret. They are with me. Ironically, we are all headed for the caves."

As he spoke, Barbizon signalled for Mantulu to get the torn remnant of the girl's dress that had obviously been ripped off of her by the pursuing jaguar and lay on the ground near the tree in which she had eagerly sought refuge. They all knew the young woman as Lana, who lived in a nearby village, and her lack of concern at being naked was simply part of the Karoo culture which had no sense of shame when it came to the naked body, unlike the so-called civilized world where the paragons of virtue always pointed the finger of condemnation.

Barbizon then introduced Larry to Mantulu, while Danny seemed to ignore them all, as he was fascinated by Lana.

Lynton, pointing at the AK-47's said, "That is a lot of firepower for a scientific expedition."

"Hey," exclaimed Danny, still staring at Lana, "you never know, whether you are in the streets of an American city or the wilds of Africa, when you might run into a beast. I am always prepared. This is just insurance. However, it sure wasn't worth the premium this time though," he added disgustedly; "jammed on me right when I needed it the most. But say, you were there all right. I gotta hand it to you. You're something else, mister, and if I can ever return the favour just let me know."

Barbizon nodded his appreciation of the offer and said, with conviction, "Thanks, but I find guns are a detriment to mankind. Rarely have they ever solved a problem."

Danny, a typical American gun lover, offered his view. "Ain't never seen a situation that a gun couldn't help even things up."

Lynton offered her take on the comment. "Well, for far too many Americans, guns are the problem, not the solution."

Lana offered her observational analysis, "Seems like Barbizon's weapon was a bit more dependable this time than your guns. Still, I thank each of you for saving my life."

Danny, who had not taken his eyes off the beautiful Lana, said "Mighty welcome missy."

While all the pleasantries were being exchanged, Lynton was wondering what the radiation mentioned by Larry might have to do with the strange occurrences at the Baldasack Caves. Thus, that tapestry of fate was still being completed. Without realizing it, all those present were part of the tapestry. They were the threads that would unwittingly stitch together the coming terror that was waiting to be unleashed.

Chapter 4

I Will Love Being Your Guide

The domino of fate strikes down angels,
Whose wings are laden with radiation.
The winds of evil blow across the Karoo;
Even God could not perform mediation.

In a world where sanity is shredded,
And flowers of peace are trampled,
Darkness hides the light of hope,
As evil is about to be sampled.

Hearts of compassion are smashed.
Fate is dancing about with glee,
While the darkness engulfs the light,
And sanity prepares to flee.

There are forces at play in the world, which few, if any, can truly comprehend, and the tempest

91

that swirls about in the tumultuous sea of evil that has a firm grip on mankind is always toying with fate and that tapestry that is being carefully woven over time is sometimes interrupted, but rarely stayed. To fully understand what is about to occur in the Karoo, we must go far back in time when South Africa was discovered by the white man, and its black people eventually made slaves of an evil system called apartheid.

The history of South Africa starts more than 100,000 years ago, when the first humans inhabited the region. The historical record of this ethnically diverse country is generally divided into five distinct periods: the pre-colonial era, the colonial era, the post-colonial era, the apartheid era, and the post-apartheid era. Much of this history, particularly of the colonial and post-colonial eras, is characterized by extreme clashes of culture, incredibly violent territorial disputes between European settlers and indigenous people, dispossession and repression, and other racial and political tensions.

Lynton's South African Adventure:
Demon of Fire at the Karoo Escarpment

The discoveries of diamonds and gold in the 19th century had a profound effect on the fortunes of the region, introducing a shift away from an exclusively agrarian-based economy towards industrialization and the development of urban infrastructure. The discoveries also led to new conflicts culminating in open warfare between the Boer (primarily Dutch) settlers and imperial Britain, fought essentially for control over the South African mining industry.

Following the defeat of the Boers in the Anglo-Boer or South African War (1899–1902), the Union of South Africa was created with the Afrikaans in firm control of the nation, though bowing to British sovereignty. It was during this era that the eventual World War II icon of freedom, Winston Churchill, set up concentration camps in South Africa to imprison the whites he thought were a threat to the British Empire. Hitler's Third Reich used Churchill's camps and America's Indian Reservations as models for the concentration camps in Germany and Poland.

Lynton's South African Adventure:
Demon of Fire at the Karoo Escarpment

From 1948 to 1994, South African politics were dominated by Afrikaner nationalism centered on racial segregation and white minority rule known officially as apartheid, an Afrikaans word meaning separateness. It was an extension of segregationist legislation enacted prior to 1934. In 1994, after decades of armed struggle and international opposition to apartheid, the liberation group known as the African National Congress (ANC) achieved victory in the country's first democratic election. Today, the repressive past, thanks to the non-retributive leadership of the dominant blacks, has seen a cohesive, all-inclusive society arise out of the ashes of the evil system called apartheid.

From its inception, South Africa was a land that saw the whites control the country while relegating the blacks and other races to subservient status. It is not our purpose here to explore the early history, but rather to develop some rudimentary knowledge about what led to Harry Smith, Eric Kabowski, Agus, Danny

Dampier and Larry Hannover to be part of that grand tapestry of fate that was reaching its apex.

Apartheid as an officially structured policy was introduced after the general election of 1948. Legislation classified inhabitants into four racial groups: black, white, coloured and Indian and residential areas were segregated. Four million non-white South Africans were removed from their homes, and forced into segregated neighbourhoods, in one of the largest mass removals in modern history, though not on par with the USA's forced removal of Native Americans to reservations. Non-white political representation was abolished in 1970, and starting in that year, black people were deprived of their citizenship, legally becoming citizens of one of 10 tribally based self-governing homelands, four of which became nominally independent states. The government segregated education, medical care, beaches and other public services, and provided black people with services that were inferior to those of white people. Much of this was patterned after the American southern states which also had their own system of apartheid.

Significant internal resistance, violence and a long arms and trade embargo against South Africa led to a series of popular uprisings and protests which resulted in a retaliatory ban of all opposition, and the imprisonment of anti-apartheid leaders. As unrest spread and became more effective and militarized, state organizations responded with repression and violence. Along with the sanctions placed on South Africa by the international community, this made it increasingly difficult for the government to maintain the regime. However, the USA was a frequent violator of the trade bans placed on the country, and through clandestine efforts actually supported the regime out of fear that communists might come to power there and undercut the heavy U.S. corporate investments in the mining industry.

This inordinate fear of communism, for years, made the USA practice a form of terrorism based on the belief that communism had to be thwarted, so the capitalist class could continue its reign over the world. The Cold War was more an invention of the USA than the Soviet Union, as Americans were propagandized through fear-mongering to believe that an evil communist was always lurking about ready to steal their freedom. This fear led the U.S. government to indirectly support apartheid as a way to assure South Africa would be a bulwark against communist expansion into the African continent.

Agus was in his puberty during the Cold War, and he watched helplessly as his human rights were abused and repressed by an evil system that elevated one race as superior to another. Thus was born the hatred that eventually totally consumed him.

The Republic of South Africa's ambitions to develop nuclear weapons began in 1948 with the acquiescence of the USA. However, America covered up its involvement by using Israel, which was also secretly beginning a nuclear weapons program, as a conduit for nuclear technology. By

1965, American corporations like Allis-Chalmers were openly supplying research nuclear reactors.

South Africa was able to mine uranium ore domestically, and used aerodynamic nozzle enrichment techniques to produce weapons-grade material. South Africa developed a small finite deterrence arsenal of gun-type fission weapons in the 1980s. Six were constructed, according to records, but the truth is there were actually eight constructed.

The warheads were originally configured to be delivered from one of several aircraft types then in service with the South African Air Force. However, two of the bombs (numbers 7 and 8) were designed for delivery by missile or were able to be triggered by time delay mechanisms if they were placed anywhere. Though fairly large, they were small enough to be carried in a small van.

Supposedly, the weapons, by international agreement with the International Atomic Energy Agency, were to be destroyed in 1989 by a team of South African scientists led by a man named

Dieter Himmler. (Yes, he was a descendant of the infamous Heinrich Himmler of Nazi fame.) It had been consistently reported that six weapons existed, but as alluded to earlier, there were actually eight plus two partial bombs. Himmler managed to cart the two additional ones and the partially completed ones away to a secret location, and no one bothered to check for years.

In 1994, the International Atomic Energy Agency confirmed that six weapons had been destroyed and one partially completed one had also been dismantled. No mention was ever made of the two that apparently disappeared, because there was no record of them ever existing. A few months after the 1994 inspection, Himmler disappeared from sight and was never seen again.

Also, in 1994, unusual things starting happening at the Baldasack Caves, which had, for a long time now, kept the Karoo people in fear due to rumours of a demon lurking about within. These fears were solidified when a strange glow was seen coming from inside the caves.

Lynton's South African Adventure: Demon of Fire at the Karoo Escarpment

It was while Barbizon was a small child that he had seen something strange one day while playing near the caves. He had read about aliens from outer space in some books, and what he saw reminded him of some pictures from those books. An extremely strange alien-like creature appeared at the entrance to the cave. He was covered in a thick grey metallic over-garment that appeared to be pulsating with waves of infrared intensity. The helmet the creature wore was totally black, so he could not make out any facial features. He was maybe 300 feet away, but he could still feel heat coming from this creature. It made him so fearful that he ran to the village, where he was told by an elder to never again go near those caves, for within was the demon Kalma, Lord of the Underworld.

Barbizon was an astute learner, and his curiosity often got the better of him, but he had never allowed that curiosity to entice him into the Baldasack Caves. His childhood experience had caused a trauma that kept him from there.

Lynton's South African Adventure:
Demon of Fire at the Karoo Escarpment

Lynton walked slowly along the dusty path leading toward Mantulu's village which was beside a river that meandered serenely in the bottom of the ancient crater which formed the valley Baldasack. At her right walked Barbizon, and at her left the beautiful maiden, Lana. Behind them came Larry and Danny. Lynton was apprehensive. She had learned many things in her life, and one of the most important was to never accept anything at face value. There was something that bothered her about Larry. A nuclear physicist trying to explore a source of radiation made sense she supposed, but there was an uneasiness that crept into her psyche as she felt there was more to it than that.

Walking through the village, all were greeted with curiosity, save Barbizon. As they approached a large circular hut at the end of the village, there lying on a cotton blanket was a young girl of maybe 15 who was writhing in pain. She had huge red blisters on her back that were swollen with crusty dark red scabs.

The girl was weeping softly, sometimes choking down a muffled sob, while all around her exhibited pained expressions of concern. Larry looked down at her with intense interest and a determined look of recognition while all others seemed particularly puzzled.

Larry said, "Heat some lukewarm water, get any type oil, even cooking oil if necessary, and rub it on the blisters."

"What is it?" asked Lynton.

"It isn't about what it is. It is about why it is more than anything else. Was she near the Baldasack Caves when this happened?"

One of the ladies attending the girl said, "This is a girl with a curious nature. She was there yes. She was encouraged by friends to tempt the demon. She had climbed up near the lower cave, as she reached the opening, she got scared, turned around and had started back down. A big burst of red light flashed from inside the cave with such intensity that it caught her clothes on fire and burned her flesh. She ran back to the village with a few of her friends and," she then pointed at the girl's back, "this is the result. The demon is angry."

Larry looked at her and said, "Yes, the demon is angry indeed, and it is preparing for an onslaught of unimaginable evil."

Barbizon and Lynton stood side-by-side and looked at one another. Suddenly, Danny blurted out, "Let's get over there and kick some demon butt!"

Larry said, "It isn't that easy. This is a demon of incredible power. We must be very careful about approaching those caves."

Lynton, with a quizzical look directed toward Larry, said, "And why are you sure it is a demon. Are you not a scientist? Is it not a bit far-fetched for you to believe in demons?"

"Little lady, there are all kinds of demons in this world, and the demon in those caves is worse than any demon you could imagine."

Barbizon looked directly at Larry while pointing at Lynton. "This is a demon fighter."

Lynton's South African Adventure:
Demon of Fire at the Karoo Escarpment

Larry placed his hand on Barbizon's shoulder as he said, "I know this one. Lynton Viñas is famous the world over for her battles against the Aswangs in Tagaytay, the demons in Columba, exposing the charlatan in Taal Heritage Village and for attempting the impossible on Balete Drive battling two ghosts. This is a woman who has proven her metal, but she, believe me, has never tackled something this insidious."

Lynton took a deep breath and said, "You know something none of us do, and keeping it from us might not be wise."

"I cannot be sure of anything right now. I must examine the caves first. Only then can I be sure. If it is what I think it is, the whole world is at risk."

Barbizon was troubled, but looking over at Lynton said, "We can rest tonight, and tomorrow we will go to the caves. Whatever lurks about within must be confronted, before any more harm comes to the people of this village."

Larry looked over at Danny, who was next to Lana. "My friend and I are in agreement."

Lynton's South African Adventure:
Demon of Fire at the Karoo Escarpment

The injured girl seemed to be getting better, but the decision was made to take her to Cape Town in a Land Rover the next morning as Larry insisted she needed a decontamination treatment. To which Lynton interjected, "Decontamination for what?"

Larry turned to the girl's mother and said, "Take her to the Christian Barnard Hospital. They can look at the burns and take the appropriate action."

Lynton, looking into Larry's eyes, said, "She has radiation poisoning."

Larry, without confirming it verbally, just shrugged his shoulders, but Lynton knew, and she looked over at Barbizon, who also knew. Meanwhile, Danny, enthralled with Lana to the point of obsession, had no idea about what was going on around him, nor did he care.

They were all assigned huts for the evening, but Barbizon took Lynton by the hand and led her to the nearby river as he said, "I need to talk to you privately."

The quiet by the river was peaceful and relaxing as the two of them sat on an old tree stump. Barbizon, a look of worry on his face, said, "You know something I don't."

"Not really," replied Lynton. "I do suspect something though, and, if I am right, you do not need a demon hunter. You need someone far more skilled than I am. Larry is, no doubt, the one who can solve this problem."

Barbizon was a virile young man, and though he had never experienced even a girlfriend, he had a man's urges; consequently, he felt a strong physical attraction toward Lynton. He was inexperienced and awkward, which probably accounted for his impetuousness as illustrated by his sudden move toward her, grabbing her around the waist and clumsily kissing her.

Lynton could not deny that she found the man attractive, but she was committed entirely to Wayne, and though she allowed a short, gentle kiss, she slowly pushed him away and said, "This is inappropriate."

Barbizon was humiliated and remorseful for his impetuous actions. "I am sorry, so sorry. I did not mean offence. You see, I have never been with a woman, and I find you so attractive, so sweet and so alluring."

As he hung his head in shame, Lynton, kind hearted and sympathetic as always, reached out and placed her right hand on his left shoulder. "Do not be ashamed of your feelings. They are natural, and if I were not attached romantically to another, I might be more receptive. You shall find that special person one day, and she will be lucky to have such a fine man to care for her."

Barbizon was humbled, but his ardour was not staid. He smiled and said, "I shall not give up on you."

Lynton replied, "You are a man of towering intellect with superb physical attributes. Believe me, you can find better than me. Look for someone who will compliment you, someone who is familiar with your way of life and can adjust to living in the wilds."

Lynton's South African Adventure: Demon of Fire at the Karoo Escarpment

Barbizon pointed to a tree house in the distance. "That is where I call home. Come and stay the night there. I shall sleep on the floor and you shall have the bed. I promise to not be impetuous as I was before."

Lynton smiled, took his hand and said, "I'll be glad to spend the night in your home."

Barbizon said to Lynton
I know you're a tender soul
But now that you're in Africa
You have to play a different role

The elephants and the monkeys
Will be your new found friends
Living here in the wild
The excitement never ends

You'll like my tree house
With monkey Chipper by your side
Try starting a new life
I will love being your guide

Chapter 5

It Was About Lana

That night Lynton slept peacefully high in a tree. In the morning, the birds were chirping and she arose expecting to see Barbizon on the floor fast asleep as it was still dark out, but he was gone. She got up, and in the glistening moonlight went over to the large bookshelves that surrounded the one room home. She saw there books by Hemingway, Goethe, Steinbeck, Hawking and a host of others, indicating that he was extremely well-read. Then, a smile pursed her lips as she saw *Lynton Curls Her Hair, Lynton Buys a New Cell-Phone and Hears the Voice of Doom, Lynton and the Vampire at Tagaytay Manor, Lynton Walks on Water,* and all the other Wayne Frye books.

109

As she strolled about, she thought how pleased Wayne would be to know that his books were read in the wilds of the Karoo. As all humans do, she felt the need to use the washroom, but there appeared to be nowhere for one to relieve themselves.

She saw a small anti-room to one side with three or four steps leading downward. She peered in and saw a rudimentary washroom. There was a hole cut in the floor that was connected to a long pipe running downward toward the ground where a large pit was dug. Above, to her left was a large catchment tank for collecting water and under it a shower nozzle. It was crude, but no worse than she remembered as a child living in the far provinces of the Philippines.

While Lynton was busying herself in the tree house, Barbizon had gone outside to gather eggs from the chicken coop he kept below. As he was gathering up the eggs, his keen ears heard a sound in the brush off to his left down by the river which was maybe 100 feet below.

Lynton's South African Adventure:
Demon of Fire at the Karoo Escarpment

Lynton's ears were less keen than Barbizon's, but she, too, heard something. She went over to the opening to the tree house and looked out to see several shadows were moving about down by the river. She noticed Barbizon moving in their direction. She felt uneasiness, an apprehension that something was wrong.

Suddenly, she saw perhaps ten men surround Barbizon. There was a furious fight and the men were being tossed about as he fended them off. She quickly grabbed the rope attached to the tree and scurried down to run to the village for help. When she got to the bottom, she was met by four men who grabbed her, pulling her hands behind her back and binding them. She tried kicking at their shins, but they laughed as they viciously slapped her across the face, nearly knocking her unconscious as she heard Barbizon fighting with the others down by the river.

Lynton had been close to death many times and from her appearance, their attitude toward her made it not difficult for her to imagine that they would require but the slightest pretext to destroy her. What their intentions might be was highly problematical, though she could conceive of but one motive, which was ransom. Yes, she deduced that she was being kidnapped.

Agus spoke to her in perfect English. "Resist and you die. Scream and you die."

With those words, they appeared uninterested in what was going on down by the river, as they quickly whisked her toward a nearby hill. Entering a narrow rocky canyon, the trail wound steeply upward as they trudged onward to a small, level mesa, at the lower end of caves that appeared to be in the shape of a skull. She had never seen them, but she knew from instinct that she was at the Baldasack Caves.

As they neared the caves, Lynton discovered that their approach had been made beneath the scrutiny of lookouts posted all about, hiding in the scrub as their heads and shoulders were now plainly visible as the band marched forward toward the caves. These sentries came out of hiding and were shouting greetings and queries to the members of the returning band as there seemed great euphoria that they had a hostage in tow. Although there was nothing particularly menacing in the attitude of the throng gathered, there was a definite unfriendliness in their demeanour that cast a further gloom of apprehension upon the already depressed spirits of Lynton. Also, they were all dressed in fatigues worn by military personnel, and they wore a patch on the left shoulder which Lynton, with limited knowledge of Arabic, was able to decipher with the relative ease of a novice.

alwala' li'asama

Translation:

Loyalty to Osama

A tall white man, wearing what looked like a space suit, emerged from the lower cave entrance and waved his hand. Those there all shouted with glee apparently in praise of he who was, no doubt, their master.

There was no smile upon the face of the helmeted man as he very sternly addressed Lynton, who stood with her hands still bound behind her back. "You are the demon fighter are you not?"

"I am a woman who stands against demons of evil, if that is what you mean," replied a defiant Lynton.

The man eyed her intently for some time, as though attempting to read the innermost secrets of her mind, before he spoke again. "My men are complete total fools. They were specifically instructed to bring the one who is by the side of the woman - to bring Barbizon."

"Well, do not chastise them too much. Maybe you are the fool. Perhaps it takes a fool to give orders to a fool."

He did not seem particularly amused by her response, but apparently upon reflection, realized the error in his instructions. "I apologize for the inconvenience to which my men have put you," as he motioned for her to climb up to the cave.

Lynton's South African Adventure:
Demon of Fire at the Karoo Escarpment

She walked into a cave that was so dark she could not make out its contents until the man turned on the light atop the helmet he was wearing. He pointed to another pile of garments that looked like a space suit and said, "You would be well-advised to put those garments on. You are coming with me. Any arguments and you will pay a heavy price. We understand one another?"

As she moved to the garments and started to put them on, she said, "I understand, yes."

After suiting up, the man said, "I am Dieter Himmler, and I am master here of all you survey, and all those men are loyal to me without fault. They live in the upper caves where we have built a gigantic underground city. This cave in which we now stand is our work cave. It is the heart of a plan instituted 25 years ago to bring a world that has lost its way to its senses the only way possible. You shall be amazed demon hunter at just what has been accomplished here. I became a loyal devotee of Nazism over 50 years ago, and I am here to proclaim the glory of Adolph Hitler."

The ten men who accosted Barbizon had paid a heavy price. Three lay dead by the river and the rest had scurried back with various wounds to the caves. Agus had been chastised by Himmler for his incompetence, but when he insisted on returning to the village of the Karoo to accomplish his mission, he was told there would be no need, as with them having the woman, Barbizon would be upon them soon and they should lay a trap for him and those who would be accompanying him.

Forty men formed a well-organized party led by Barbizon and Mantulu. All were struggling up the steep slopes of the Karoo range a few kilometres to the east. Larry and Danny had joined them.

As they made their way steadily forward, Larry noticed a huge sink hole off to his left and asked Barbizon how long it had been there. He replied, "Before I was born. There was a great explosion here."

Mantulu interjected, "A good 25 years at least. I was a teenager, and remember a great rumbling

116

noise and an earthquake that shook the village violently."

The intensity of Larry's interest was obvious. "And was there a prolonged rumbling of the earth, not a shaking, so much as a rolling feeling?"

Mantulu replied, "Yes, a rolling feeling, like you were riding a wave. And the sound was muffled like when you cup your hands over your ears."

Barbizon was well read enough to figure out where Larry was leading with his questions. He said, "You think there was a nuclear explosion here?"

"I am afraid so my friend. My mission here is to locate the source of that radiation, and I surmise that radiation has been here for a very long time, but for some reason was never picked up until now." He turned to Mantulu and said, "And there have been many people getting sick over the years, and dying mysteriously, especially children and the old."

"Yes, many," offered Mantulu.

"We may need the help of the authorities, but first we must be sure of what we are facing."

Mantulu was adamant when he said, "We do not want the outside world here. We have a wonderful life, and it is protected by the escarpment."

Larry said, "I am afraid you may have no choice if my speculations prove true."

They entered the barren scrub forest and there the going became more difficult, for the ground rose rapidly; and the underbrush was thick. Still, they relentlessly fought their way upward. Barbizon was frantic, as he feared for Lynton's life.

As Barbizon led the group forward toward the caves, Lynton and Himmler reached an area with huge thick solid lead doors at least ten feet thick. Himmler pushed a large bolt to the left and the doors screeched open. He turned to her and said, "You may remove your garments now as this is a safe area we are entering. Only outside these doors do you face the demon of fire."

Lynton's South African Adventure:
Demon of Fire at the Karoo Escarpment

Lynton removed her protective garments and, with her guide, edged further back into the cave, maybe at least a kilometre. Though somewhat fearful at what lay ahead for her, the light of hope beat within the bosom of the dynamic dynamo. Moving further and further into the cave, the darkness connoted shallow evil concealing cruel and treacherous depths of depravity while an outside world was already filled with the depravity of social and economic injustice. She shuddered as she approached the back of the cave where a huge well-lit cavern opened up, and a bevy of workers were buzzing about laboriously involved in their duties. This was a cave that was hiding cruelty and treachery beneath the surface of the Great Karoo Escarpment. She glanced at the faces of the workers who were all singularly preoccupied with their work, and she was frightened at what they represented – an evil of monumental proportions.

In a deep side cave to her right, she saw an abominable sight. Maybe 50 women were chained to the walls and, though beautiful, appeared to be in a complete discombobulated state of distress. Half clothed, they were obviously there for the pleasure of the men. Her guide pointed in their direction and said, "You shall join them soon, but allow me to show you what you think is a demon, and indeed it is a demon, many demons that will rain terror down upon those who defeated my grandfather and had the nerve to put on trial those who simply wanted an end to Jewry."

Connecting those words to his last name, she immediately knew which Himmler was his grandfather. This was no doubt the son of Heinrich Himmler's own illegitimate son. Sometimes, the effect of genes can be horrendous, and in this man of maybe 60, beat the heart of an ardent supporter of a group of the most abominable cretins to ever walk the earth. This was a man who embraced the Nazi doctrine of supremacy that sent millions of Jews, homosexuals, gypsies and the deformed to the concentration camps and burned them in ovens of evil to glorify the white Aryan race.

Lynton's South African Adventure:
Demon of Fire at the Karoo Escarpment

Perhaps some detail on Dieter Himmler's grandfather might be conducive to a better understanding of what Lynton was up against. Heinrich Luitpold Himmler was Reichsführer of the Schutzstaffel (Protection Squadron; SS), and a leading member of the Nazi Party of Germany. Adolf Hitler appointed him a military commander and General Administrator of the entire Third Reich. Himmler was one of the most powerful men in Nazi Germany and one of the men most directly responsible for the Holocaust.

Himmler had a lifelong interest in occultism, interpreting Germanic neo-pagan beliefs to promote the racial policy of Nazi Germany. His affair in 1936 with Lydia Oldencoff produced a son named Erich, who, after the war immigrated with his mother to South Africa, where he married and had a son in 1956 with a Dutch woman. He named the boy Dieter Heinrich, in honour of his grandfather. Erich was an engineer and his son Dieter followed in his footsteps, receiving his doctorate at the age of 23 from University of Cape

Town. Dieter was a great supporter of apartheid and believed that such a system would make South Africa a vanguard in what he saw as the mongrelisation of humanity through inter-ethnic marriage. With his beliefs as a guide, he eagerly joined the effort to develop a South African nuclear arsenal. Ironically, the effort would see him collaborate with the Jews he had been taught to hate, because Israel was a conduit for American nuclear technology intended to assist South Africa in the battle against communism, which was an American obsession.

As Lynton moved forward, she noticed on the walls of the cave large portraits of Adolph Hitler at the height of his glory that had enthralled a nation to the xenophobia that would lead it to destruction. Yet, among the workers were blacks and obviously Muslims. This seemed an unusual conglomeration of adherents to a cause that was oriented toward promulgating Aryan (white & blue eyed as the norm) superiority. But the pursuit of evil makes for many anomalies.

Lynton's South African Adventure:
Demon of Fire at the Karoo Escarpment

It is impossible to understand why people seem hell-bent on working against their own self-interests. In the USA, the uneducated poor whites tend to vote Republican, despite that party's penchant for supporting the wealthy and demonizing those at the bottom of the economic ladder. They are easily swayed by patriotism, and fear that the other political party will come after their guns or keep them from praying to the Jesus they all adore. In other parts of the world, the same techniques are used to keep those who represent the wealthy in power, often through religion that hurls vindictive hate about like it was a panacea for all the evil that abounds. Unfortunately, the truth is that religion itself often traps people in an ever downward spiral into judgmental arrogance that does not embrace compassion. Muslims and Blacks were working for Himmler, because they were all trapped by a skilled practitioner of brainwashing, who had successfully swayed them into believing he offered them redemption and retribution.

Lynton's South African Adventure:
Demon of Fire at the Karoo Escarpment

Lynton was no fool, she was an astute observer of the human psyche, and she knew that Himmler was enjoying showing her his power, and sharing with her his designs for an obvious cataclysmic event to humble the world before him. He was like a man she had seen often on American television, a businessman who revelled in the mention of his very own name. Every thing he built, every business he started bore his name, as if the very sight of his own name brought him orgasmic pleasure. Himmler was no different. He was not well-known now, but one could sense that he was relishing the coming calamity that would put his name on the tongue tips of billions. He glorified in the evil he was about to unleash. Still, Lynton knew not what the evil was, but she suspected. In fact, she suspected it from the very instant she heard that Larry Hannover was in the Karoo to check on some mysterious radiation emanating from the area. There was a demon in the caves alright, but it was a demon manufactured by a demon, the worst demon of them all – man.

Lynton's South African Adventure:
Demon of Fire at the Karoo Escarpment

As Lynton moved with great trepidation ever farther into the cave, the party led by Barbizon was now almost to the caves and about to encounter an impediment. The lovely Lana, much to the joy of Danny, came tooling up to the party on an ATV, motor humming like a cannon firing in the barren terrain they were traversing. She shouted, "They are marching your way. They plundered the village and now plan to destroy you before you reach the caves. I managed to escape to warn you."

Barbizon, motioning for one of the warriors to give her water, said, "Who plundered the village and who is pursuing us?"

"I know not who it is. But I know they are all white men, well-equipped with powerful guns, and there are at least 100 or 200 of them. They also wear these on their shirt sleeves." She then knelt down and drew the following in the dust:

Barbizon had read many books about World War II and immediately recognized the symbol as did Larry. However, Danny looked puzzled, so Larry said, "It is the symbol of the Waffen SS that guarded the concentration camps in the Third Reich. They were Germany's most brutal troops."

Danny gripped his gun tighter and said as he looked at Lana, "They ain't so tough if I get 'um in my sights."

Though his manner was crude, Lana felt he was directing his remarks to her as a way of saying, "I'll protect you."

Mantulu said, "We cannot fight against that many. We are far too outnumbered. What do you suggest Barbizon?"

Barbizon looked at Larry and said, "You know what the problem is, and it is not important that you share it with us, as all I am concerned about is freeing Lynton from those who captured her, but you must let us know if we can defeat them. Are their weapons so superior that we cannot hope to come out victorious?"

"If the man who rules the cave has what I think he has, there are no weapons superior to what he has. The demon you fear in that cave is a demon that can engulf the whole world in the fires of hell, bring the entire earth into disarray and literally destroy almost all life as we know it. Those who now pursue us are here from a training camp in an isolated area of Namibia." He then looked at Lana, as he continued. "They dropped from the sky did they not?"

"Yes, there were two planes and the men drifted down under large white sheets and immediately began firing randomly, killing many as they demanded to know where the white man Hannover was."

Larry bowed his head, "I am so sorry. My mission was supposed to be kept secret, but obviously these men are what MI-6 Intelligence Service picked up wind of a few months ago. They are right wing fanatical Germans who seek to reconstitute the Third Reich and finish what Hitler started. They are allied with the Russian leader as an adjunct to his designs to reconstitute the Soviet Union, and he is allying himself with this highly secret SS organization. You see, there is a man here in South Africa whom we know as a brilliant scientist, and if my suspicions are confirmed, the entire world is on the brink of Armageddon if he is not stopped."

Again, Danny looked puzzled. Larry explained. "Armageddon, it is the Biblical term for, literally, the end of the world, the final battle between good and evil. The only problem with the modern world of politics is that it is difficult to define good and evil, since it often seems it is evil and the lesser evil as the only real choices."

Barbizon stood thinking of Lynton and her predicament. If he could but get among those coming their way, where they could not use firearms against him, because of the danger that they might kill members of their own party, he felt that, by virtue of his superior strength, speed and agility, he might fight his way to one of the caves where he could have a fair chance to rescue

Lynton. His companion pet monkey, Chipper, stood by his side. He sensed the worry in him, reached down and patted his forehead as he said, "First priority is to rescue Lynton. Let us," then he pointed to his left, "Veer off this direction where there are thickets in which we can hide for the night. There we will lay low and let the soldiers pass, and then, I will reconnoitre. I shall observe what is in the cave, come back and then we will plan an assault." He looked at Larry and continued, "You may come with me to confirm that whatever it is you want to confirm, is indeed there. I shall rely on your scientific knowledge to assess the dangers within."

They pushed Lana's ATV off into a deep gulley and quickly moved toward the scrub brush where they would stay until the soldiers went by and Barbizon and Larry could see what was in the caves.

Lana stayed close to Danny, as she felt safe by his side. For his part, Danny, for the first time in his life, actually felt that someone was worth protecting. It was no longer about the money he had been promised. It was about protecting Lana from harm.

Chapter 6

Nailing Someone to the Cross

The soldiers moved by not noticing the band of warriors in hiding, and as they goose-stepped with arrogant pride at their near obliteration of a village filled with peaceful people, there was no remorsefulness over the innocents they had slaughtered. This was the way of a world that equated raw power with righteousness. Every drone strike by the USA, every invasion of a sovereign nation to bring democracy was just another recruiting tool for the miscreants of mayhem who roused people against the evil of a nation where greed was promoted as an enviable trait. The hypocrisy was what made so many enemies for America, and now this group was going to send a message of hate in return.

131

Lynton's South African Adventure:
Demon of Fire at the Karoo Escarpment

Oddly, an American businessman in cahoots with the Russian leader was about to use the Aryan idea of supremacy in conjunction with ISIS and Al Qaeda to garner more riches while the Russian leader would get the power he craved.

As the group lay quietly, making sure the troops had passed; Danny asked Lana how she survived the massacre. She sighed and told the story exactly as it happened. "We were going about our daily routine when three huge propeller driven planes suddenly appeared on the horizon above the escarpment. At first, we were all fascinated when the skies were filled with the white sheets and men were underneath them. Other sheets dropped big boxes onto the ground, and when the first men untangled themselves from the sheets, they started firing weapons that spit rapid fire at the villagers. They never asked for surrender, only kept firing until all were mowed down. I hid under the ATV which was covered by a tarp. I heard one of the men say that the mission was accomplished."

"I was frightened beyond belief as they showed no mercy whatsoever as they annihilated everyone without care, but I crawled up onto the ATV, fired it up and with bullets whizzing behind me, sped off into the bush. They had no motorized vehicles, so I managed to escape."

Danny asked Larry, "Why would they do that?"

With Barbizon listening intently, he replied, "To eliminate any impediments to what they are about to do."

Barbizon said, "And just what are they about to do?"

"As I said, they are about to unleash Armageddon."

Barbizon sighed and pressed no further, because he knew what it was, but was willing to wait for Larry's confirmation. He looked over at Danny and Mantulu. "You two stay here and wait for word from us. Our small band of fighters are probably the only chance we have to stop whatever is about to unfold, for I fear," and then he looked directly at Larry, "that our time is very short."

"It is my friend. I would say we have no more than 48 hours, because things are being set in motion as all the stars are almost perfectly aligned for what is about to occur."

In Moscow, the Russian head-of-state was on a red-line private call to a businessman in his Manhattan tower, headquarters for his far-flung empire that he had assembled over the years in attempts to prove to his father that he was worthy of the name he bore. In truth, he was a gigantic failure who had squandered more money than he made, but he fought the doubts in his abilities by being a bombastic, arrogant self-promoter whose braggadocio was legendary. Like President George Bush, who manufactured a war and sent young men and women off to die for a lie to prove to his father he was a man, this was an individual who was a man-child, desperately grasping for some semblance of success when the truth was he simply was a failure at every single thing he did.

His only real accomplishment was convincing people he was successful.

The Russian leader said, "My friend, it is coming to fruition."

"Thank you," said the businessman, as he pressed a button on the phonc that sent an immediate alert ring to businessmen in the United Kingdom, Belgium, Switzerland, Germany, France, Spain, Portugal, Italy, Saudi Arabia, Dubai and South Africa. All the businessmen immediately got on the line and the New York businessman simply said, "October 15 at 10:00 AM New York time." Thus a plot that had been hatched many years before was coming to its conclusion, and these privileged, arrogant, self-aggrandizing, greedy bastards were about to reap a harvest of wealth that was the result of gold hoarding all those years. Together, these 12 businessmen had privately bought up 40% of the world's supply of gold, and what was about to happen would put them in possession of nearly 100% of the gold supply once Himmler carried out a plan he had coordinated with them and the leader of Russia.

Those who worship money, power, prestige and the worldly things that shine and glisten are the biggest problem in a world with all the resources needed to feed, clothe and shelter every human being, but because the few hog all the resources, the many are left to live in the squalor of economic induced poverty. Why is it that the rich and powerful cannot see that regardless of all the wealth they may possess, the richest person in the world will suffer the same fate as we all do – death? We see here the evil of covetousness. He who places all happiness in wealth is, in the end, not a very happy person. It was once said by a wise man that the love of money is the root of all evil. Every sort of wickedness and vice, in one way or another, grows from the love of money. We cannot look around without perceiving many proofs of this, especially in a day of outward prosperity for the few while the many are in a constant, frantic struggle to keep from sinking into a sea infested with the sharks of capitalistic exploitation as represented by these 12 reprehensible men who were prepared to wreck worldwide devastation for profits.

As Lynton stood in the huge cavern that had been carved from the rock, she looked down a long corridor right in front of her. Himmler smiled, motioned for her to follow him and said, "I shall allow you to see the real demons that will bring glory to the risen Third Reich, now a Fourth Reich that will glorify the name of Hitler and make it take its place in a world that is now ready for his genius.

They walked into a huge cavern, and there before Lynton was the real evil, the real demon in the form of two huge bombs. She knew what they were. They were atomic bombs. They were the two bombs that had supposedly been destroyed, and beside them was a third - the one that had not been finished, now, miniaturized to suitcase size, now completed and ready to unleash its massive destructive power. She looked up on the wall at a huge electronic map and knew instantly what Himmler's plan was to wrap the world in the arms of evil.

There was a map of the USA and a red "X" was placed prominently over Fort Knox, Kentucky. The other "X" on the USA portion of the map was over Liberty Street in Manhattan and the initials FRB were scribed there, which she deduced to mean Federal Reserve Bank. It did not take a person of immense intelligence to deduce that those two bombs were destined for those two places where the USA stored all its gold reserves. A direct hit or air burst from a nuclear weapon would render the gold, even if it was not incinerated, useless for a thousand years and totally collapse the U.S. economy.

Himmler could see the wheels turning in Lynton's head. "You have it figured demon fighter. Yes, we will obliterate the gold supply of the biggest terrorist nation on earth. Our strike will be more devastating than the blow delivered by Osama. It will put the final nail in the coffin of a nation that keeps proclaiming its exceptionalism while it forces its grotesque corporate, rich coddling capitalism on the whole world."

Lynton sighed and replied, "I am no capitalist, because I see its inherent evil, but George Bush proved the ineffectiveness of fighting evil with evil. He created more evil than he destroyed."

At that point Agus came up and said, "You have no idea of real evil, until you have endured a system of racism as I did when I was young. When these bombs are released over America, it will be small repayment for aggrandizing that buffoon Reagan who labelled Mandela a terrorist while embracing the architects of apartheid. And here, in South Africa, I will be free, with Himmler's help, to bring those evil minions of despair who were allowed to be freed from prosecution for their evil to justice. I shall wreck havoc upon them and finally exact retribution."

At that point, Himmler motioned for two other men to join them. Thus, the dynamic dynamo was introduced to Harry Smith and Eric Kabowski.

She sensed an evil countenance in them as they both stared at her in a lustful manner. However, it was more than that – there was an aura of intense evil that appeared to emanate deep within their souls.

To be attacked by merciless beasts in the wild was one thing, but to be mercilessly attacked with evil intentions as was displayed by these men was indeed the apex of evil that she genuinely feared. Fortunately, she had a champion of determination on her side, because Barbizon and Larry were making their way toward the caves.

From the safety of a nearby mesa, Barbizon glanced up the face of the cliff that was shaped like a skull and formed the caves. Several men were digging a hole at the center of a circular space. Upon the ground was a wooden cross.

Larry was horror stricken. He looked quizzically at Barbizon. Were they going to perpetrate the horrible atrocity of nailing someone to the cross?

Chapter 7

More Likely to be Food than to Eat Food

Tapestry engraved with lines

That cut deeply into life,

Stipulating endless journeys,

Marking heavens and hells

Alongside freeways of hope and misery,

Speeding breakneck toward hot flames

Stipulated by that which is predetermined,

Freehandedly drawn by invisible hands

Sewing fate, after fate, after fate!

Many main roads guide tomorrow,

As signposts direct, determining course,

Until clouds gather and storms quicken.

Winds swell into an erupting tempest,

And deviate the course of reckoning

141

Lynton's South African Adventure:
Demon of Fire at the Karoo Escarpment

Into the unknown realm,

While roads become quagmires

Drown in tears of lost opportunity

Evolved by fate's unexpected storms.

Instead of being on the freeway of hope,

You found a place where dreams drown.

Fate has put you on a rocky road

Slowly propelling you relentlessly along,

As another thread etches into your fate

Gently fondling your life's lines,

Ordering them to somehow make sense,

Embracing each one, giving it a place

Wherein they all should fit into your fate.

All your lines lie in front of you,

And you must never ever look back,

As something might be gaining on you.

For woven together on the tapestry,

The silver threads of fate stitch the road

That leads to the distant horizon,

Where an outcome has waited patiently.

142

Lynton's South African Adventure:
Demon of Fire at the Karoo Escarpment

Tarry not in the land of lost hope

For your life is a tapestry of fate....

That tapestry which is sown delicately with precision by the threads of fate was slowly and assuredly gathering about the Baldasack Caves. Not only did the fate of the Great Karoo and South Africa rest in Himmler's evil hands, but the fate of the world was now at play in the fields of discontent that Lynton found herself unexpectedly in. She contemplated the intense reality of what was about to occur. She had faced the supernatural without fear, but there was nothing supernatural about this evil, or so she assumed, until Himmler motioned for her to come with him to a dark corner. He guided her to an opening that led down a dark corridor. He moved closer to her and whispered, "I decided another fate for you. Guess what's at the end of the corridor?"

"I am sure I do not know," replied Lynton.

Smiling, Himmler whispered, "The devil – the demon of the Karoo who eats little brown Filipino girls for dessert."

Himmler then gave her a mighty shove into the dark chamber, forcing her to fall down onto the warm ground as he slammed lead doors shut behind her. The darkness was overwhelming. It seemed to envelope her in a never ending fortress of evil that could be felt, if not seen. Her breathing slowed as she tried to take in more of the stale, humid air that smelled of decay. She used the rough cave wall with her right hand to guide her forward. She could hear a soft dripping noise as dew slid off the rocks - drip, drip, drip, like a heartbeat. Spires of rock hung from the ceiling and others stood erect upon the floor. The chilly draft sent shivers down her spine as she edged forward toward a very bright red glow in the distance. With each step nearer the red glow, her eyes became more acclimated to the cave and slowly her vision became sharper as she honed in on the glow that was now no more than 100 feet away. It was not just fire, but rather, it seemed to be a steady flow like a volcano spewing hot, molten lava skyward from its core.

Lynton's South African Adventure:
Demon of Fire at the Karoo Escarpment

The floor dropped rapidly until it was inclined at an angle that made progress difficult; and at the same time it narrowed, giving evidence that it might be rapidly pinching out. There was now a narrow passageway as she squeezed forward between the walls when the fissure ahead of her became suddenly shrouded in gloom. Glancing up in search of an explanation of this new phenomenon, Lynton discovered that the walls far above were converging, until directly above her there was a small streak of sky visible through a tiny opening maybe 100 feet overhead. However, it was just too far above and the walls too slippery for her to entertain any hope of reaching the opening and getting to safety.

As she pushed on, the going, while still difficult because of the steepness of the floor, was improved to some extent by the absence of jumbled rocks underfoot, the closed ceiling of the corridor having offered no crumbling rim to the raging elements of the ages; but presently another handicap made itself evident, renewed darkness as the glow decreased steadily with each few yards until she was groping her way blindly, though none the less determinedly, toward the unknown that lay ahead.

That an abyss might yawn beyond her next step may have occurred to her, but she ignored the simplest considerations of safety as she continued forward. This was the fearless dynamic dynamo.

Suddenly, the red fiery glow again shot up and a voice rumbled forth from below the fire reverberating off the cave walls. "Come forward into the flames, embrace me demon hunter, and let me devour you in an all encompassing power that will warm you so you can delight in the glory of evil. I have solidified the power of Himmler and his henchman just as I did for his idol Adolph Hitler. Adolph failed because the world was united against him, but the world is more divided now, and filled with those who worship at the feet of the exalted one himself, Beelzebub, whom I gratefully serve. Come my little beauty and embrace evil with gusto." Was she hallucinating now?

Lynton's South African Adventure:
Demon of Fire at the Karoo Escarpment

Lynton had faced numerous demonic manifestations and never cowered in fear before them. She wasn't sure this was a real demon, even assuming it might be nothing more than an elaborate ruse being orchestrated by Himmler. She bellowed: "I know you Cimeries, or as you are known here, Kalma. I fear you not, for death does not make me quiver. I bow before no evil, and am unrepentant in my devotion to fighting it. So, come forth from your liar and face me you cretin of the crematorium of foulness that hides in the bowels of the earth. You are worse than the excrement that festers in the noonday sun. I spit upon you, spit upon the evil you represent."

Lynton, though never convinced that demons were real, knew from exhaustive research that supposedly riling the entities with words to lure them out of their lairs would render them less effective when not confined to the safety of their sanctuaries of evil. Suddenly, the anger of Kalma, or whatever was down there, caused the earth to shake as the flames shot upward with a fury and debris started falling from overhead as Lynton leaned to her right dropping to her knees while covering her head with her hands. She observed the area to her right and started worming her way through an aperture that was exceedingly small for the average human to fit through but her 5:2, 50 Kilo (110 pounds) body made it through with relative ease. She was glad that she had been on a diet for a few weeks. She saw a light in the far distance as she crawled ever forward, feeling the hot hair behind her as a result of the intense heat from the pit of fire, and a moment later she stood erect in astonished contemplation of the scene before her. She found herself standing near the base of a lofty mesa overlooking a scrub brush filled valley that she recognized immediately as the crater of a long extinct volcano. Below her spread a panorama of rolling, dust-dotted landscape, broken by occasional huge outcroppings of weathered lava rock; and in the center a blue lake danced in the rays of an afternoon sun.

Lynton's South African Adventure:
Demon of Fire at the Karoo Escarpment

Unbeknownst to Lynton, a harrowing drama was unfolding on the opposite site of the valley, where Barbizon and Larry were observing a horrific scene, as preparations for a crucifixion were being completed. While Lynton was struggling to make her way back to the opposite side of the valley, to trace her steps back from the front of the caves, the four men preparing the cross were now just standing, looking up toward the caves, obviously waiting for someone to bring the victim down from the hillside.

There was also another development, as a heavy excavating machine and a large dirt compactor were moving toward the caves, and it was obvious the machine had been actively compacting the landing strip for a plane, and the biggest surprise of all was the large Boeing 727 airplane that was at the end of a dirt runway of maybe 10,000 feet. It was a towering and impressive sight in the middle of nowhere. It was also an indication that something very big was about to be loaded onto it.

At the mouth of one of the caves was a large hoist being assembled to obviously lower something fairly large. Larry and Barbizon stared at each other in disbelief. Then, they looked back down at the cross and both men sighed when four men emerged from one of the cave openings with a bound victim. Barbizon's heart nearly exploded. The person of maybe 50 they had in tow was white, and he cut a towering figure of manhood. He was at least 6:5 with an incredibly muscular body that was readily on display as he was only wearing slightly above the knee shorts and nothing else. His hair was tinted with grey, but was thick and cascaded over his broad shoulders. His pectoral muscles seemed to flex with each stride, and his washboard abs flexed in a defiant way with each long stride he took. He had a rectangular face with a sturdy jaw line; his eyes were deep set under thick brows spaced evenly apart. The sharp features of the face reflected the tautness of his body structure. Oh, but on those lips, slightly pursed, one could see a defiance as there was an ever so slight grin that seemed to say, "I have no fear of you."

One could sense that he knew full-well the pain that waited in that circle down below the caves, but there was not any inkling whatsoever that he was in awe of these men or fearful of what he was about to face. In fact, one could sense the disdain and contempt he held for those who were about to kill him.

Larry looked over at Barbizon and was shocked to see tears in his eyes. He whispered, "What is it?"

Sighing, Barbizon, still with teary eyes, replied, "It is my father."

Shocked at the revelation overwhelmed Larry as he said, "What are we to do?

"My friend, I came here to rescue Lynton, but now there is another I must rescue, too. We have very little time. I shall free him, and then we will worry about Lynton."

"Should we go back for the warriors?"

"No, we have no time. Are you a good shot?"

"Fair, yes."

"There are eight of them down there. Wait until they are about to nail him to the cross, and then pick them off one by one. I shall depend on your prowess as a marksman as I serpentine my way toward my father. Keep shooting as we make our way back here."

When facing death, one often feels exhilaration for life, as being on the brink of annihilation heightens the senses. They watched as Barbizon's father was led to the circle, and just as he was about to be nailed to the wooden cross, Barbizon leaped up and darted down the side of the mesa, waving his hands and yelling at the top of his lungs while Larry squeezed off the first round, instantly killing the man with a hammer in his right hand.

Barbizon's father, hands still tied behind his back, leaped into action. He lowered his head and rammed into the stomach of the man in front of him as he raised his rifle to return fire. He did not get off a round as Barbizon's father pummelled him to the ground, rolled off him, miraculously gripping the rifle with his feet as he lay on his back. He swung the barrel with his feet furiously across the man's face as he rolled under the feet of another, causing him to tumble to the ground as young Barbizon now raced into action, diving at one man while the others were scrambling back toward the cave as Larry systematically cut them down with precision marksmanship.

The commotion had caused a mass of armed men to appear at a cave entrance. While Barbizon and his father were running toward the mesa, Larry started shooting toward the cave, making those there less concerned with the escaping two men and more concerned with their own safety. Hands still bound tightly behind his back, Barbizon's father scrambled wearily up the hillside with his son.

There was a fury of activity below as a cadre of soldiers leaped down the side of the hillside caves and bounded toward the mesa. Barbizon turned to his father and could not find words as he unbound his hands with one flick of his knife through the plastic bindings. His father, smiling said, "You are a man my son."

They embraced as Larry said, "We need to get out of here."

Going down the backside of the mesa, they made their way near the lake as dusk settled in and then darkness. It became more and more difficult to move except at a cautious pace, since the ground was often strewn with sharp edged rocks that were not visible in the darkness. Their difficulty probably meant that their pursuers were also being slowed. As they halted to drink water from the lake, Barbizon said, "Did you see a beautiful young Asian woman in the encampment?"

"I did my son. She is no doubt dead, tossed by a man named Himmler into a cauldron of fire."

Barbizon was disheartened by his father's conjecture, but defiantly refused to accept his prognostication. "She is alive. She does not give into adversity without a fight. We need help before returning, but first must shake them off our tail, and then rendezvous with the warriors my father. How did you wind up in their camp?"

"I am afraid that I know a secret that they have kept for decades, and they were weary of exposure before their plans for conquest were put in motion. You see, I have been living in one of the caves on the backside of the mesa since I left you in despair. I have been patiently waiting for death to claim me my boy, because I do not care to go on without your mother any longer. I steered clear of them for two years, but they finally came across me when they were on an expedition to the opposite side of the mesa, in search of what they called heavy water." He then looked at Larry. "You know why they wanted heavy water I am sure, because you are here from United Kingdom to verify the truth of what is going on here, a truth that has implications for the entire world."

Larry did not hesitate. "I am, yes."

"Tell my son here about a heavy water source, which lies in the lake on the opposite side of the mesa."

In a serious tone, Larry said, "Heavy water, also called deuterium oxide, H_2O, is a form of water containing a larger than normal amount of the hydrogen isotope deuterium, also known as heavy hydrogen, rather than the more common hydrogen-1 isotope also called protium that makes up most of the hydrogen in normal water. In short, heavy water is a necessary component in the triggering of old type atomic fusion weapons."

Barbizon sighed and said, "And they are in possession of old nuclear weapons and are developing or have developed other nuclear weapons in those caves."

Barbizon's father interjected, "Yes, they have two old atomic bombs from the South African nuclear programme. They are also working on a miniaturized bomb, which I think I may have seen. It is small enough to fit into an average size suitcase."

Larry sighed and offered a dire assessment. "That is why I am here, and with your confirmation, I need not go into the caves now, as it is quite obvious what the situation is. Rather, I need to notify the authorities in the UK of the existence of these weapons so that this entire complex can be surgically struck by a commando unit. Time is of the essence, because that plane is there to pick up the bombs and, no doubt, deliver them to a location where they will be used to maximum effect."

Barbizon asked, "But if it is bombed, could the bombs they have actually go off?"

Larry, a tone of intense seriousness in his quivering voice, replied, "Yes, and radiation released. That is why it must not be struck from the air. I must get to an area with cell coverage, so that I can use my secure phone to alert MI-6."

That tapestry of fate was slowly coming into a solid pattern now that was converging from several avenues. First there were the two Barbizon's and Larry trying to escape. They were trialed about half a kilometre away by 30 commandos led by a Major Dunther. Also, edging her away along in the darkness was Lynton, and then there were the 30 warriors with Mantulu.

Barbizon and his father motioned for Larry to follow them as they scaled the mesa, dropped lightly to the ground upon the opposite side and ascended the cliff a little to the south of the lake. They were shocked when they came upon Danny and Lana at the bottom of the cliff.

"What are you doing here," asked a concerned Larry.

"I am afraid," stuttered a perturbed Danny, "that most of Mantulu's men are dead."

A look of surprise scrawled on the three men's faces, young Barbizon could only utter, "No."

"Yes!" Then Danny took a deep breath as he looked at Lana. "We managed to escape because we were engaged in a romantic interlude down by the river when we heard the shots. When we got back, a large band of the same soldiers that attacked the village earlier had captured them all after a brief fight. We remained hidden in the brush as they marched Mantulu and the nine survivors this way. We were following them, but somehow got lost when darkness arrived and we wound up here."

As Danny related the details of how he and Lana wound up at the bottom of the mesa, Lynton forged her way ever forward in the darkness. The events in the cave appeared as a dream, but she knew that the reality of her situation was no dream.

She had no idea where she was heading but she knew that death was waiting for her back at the caves. She heard many creatures of the night all about her. She reached down and picked up a sharp rock, holding it in her right hand as she continued her journey. The thought of food awoke a gnawing hunger within her and she actually smiled when she thought to herself, "I am more likely to be food than eat food."

The above are the actual bombs that were assembled by South Africa in the 1980's as part of the secret nuclear weapons programme.

Chapter 8

Tapestry of Fate was Nearing Completion

Weave, weave and spin, spin

The tapestry dances again and again.

On the tapestry is sown our fate.

All our work is to culminate.

Is evil or good raising a hand

To bring what is planned?

Intertwined with others, it is sown.

The wonders lost are never known.

Lonesome moments when contrite,

Wondering if anything comes out right.

Judgement day is approaching for all.

Oh tapestry of fate, how many will fall?

Are we the martyrs of our time?

Sowing, sowing – please be kind.

Moral fortitude tipping the scale,

Lynton's South African Adventure:
Demon of Fire at the Karoo Escarpment

Oh tapestry of fate will never fail.

Humble thoughts of each one,

Wondering what is to become.

Young Barbizon said, "There is no need to go back now. The only hope for Mantulu and Lynton is for us to rescue them, but how do we overcome an army of over 100 men? We delay and they all die, possibly nailed to a cross as they were about to do to my father. And what of the small number of well-armed soldiers pursuing us now?"

Larry sighed and said, "I can try to make it back to an area where we might get a signal, and then I could inform my superiors of what is going on. They would coordinate a raid with the South African Army, but that does not address the immediate concern of Mantulu and Lynton, and believe me, I regret your friends being in peril, but unless this situation is addressed and these bombs eliminated, there will be far greater risks and far more people incinerated by a fireball from hell. This is not about those people or even us now. This is about saving millions from annihilation."

Lynton's South African Adventure:
Demon of Fire at the Karoo Escarpment

In the scrub near this group of concerned individuals was a person with a smile slowly creeping across her face, because she had found hope of salvation, but knew caution had to be exercised, as a quick approach in the darkness might elicit a inappropriate reaction from those with guns. Danny was her immediate concern, because he was an American, and Lynton knew they were prone to shoot first and ask questions later. She lay down flat on the ground and very softly said, "It's me Lynton, don't shoot."

Young Barbizon, thrilled to hear her voice, said, as he motioned for Danny and Larry to lower their guns, "Show yourself. It is safe."

Slowly rising and strolling out of the brush in the darkness with the quarter moonlight shining dimly down, walked a goddess of loveliness. When virtue and modesty enlighten charms, the lustre of a woman like Lynton is brighter than the stars of heaven, and the influence of her power is impossible to resist. She came out of the scrub smiling. The filth of the Karoo wastelands was on her scratched and lacerated body that had endured many kilometres in the barren desert as she valiantly sought to escape from those who had brought evil into paradise. The tattered and torn clothing that partially exposed her modest but ample breasts that rose rhythmically up and down in a unison that seemed to be playing a symphony of sensuality conducted by a resurrected Leonard Bernstein in Carnegie Hall, offered a view of heaven on earth. There was purity in this woman that made beauty as relative as dark and light. On her shone a sparkling, glistening beacon of magnificence that made one realize that no matter what she wore, no matter where she was, no matter how old she became her beauty of mind, body and spirit would always brighten the darkness.

All there gasped in surprise as Lynton defiantly and boldly walked up to them. Having heard all they had discussed, she said, as she shook hands with Barbizon's father, "Isn't it about time we kicked Himmler's butt?"

"Any suggestions about how we go about that," said Larry.

"There is a back entrance, but it is very narrow but maybe Lana and I can get through. I am not sure about the rest of you. I know where the bombs are, and if we can get the lead doors open, I can show you. Then Larry, you, I am sure can defuse and destroy them. Hopefully, we may be able to rescue Mantulu also, as well as about 50 women they are holding hostage."

"I can destroy the weapons, yes," replied Larry, who then took a deep breath and continued, "But rescuing Mantulu and the women I shall leave to more physically adroit men than I am."

Barbizon said, "Right now, we have about 30 men pursuing us. First, we must deal with them. Then we will figure a way into that chamber."

Lynton, with steely determination, said, "Come back with me then, and we shall see what means we can use to get into the chamber, and I saw something on my way here that may take care of your pursuers."

165

"Done," replied young Barbizon, as he stared back in the direction from which Lynton had come.

Old Barbizon said, "We can get in easily, because each day at noon, Himmler plays a game to keep the Muslims and the natives in fear. He has them convinced there is a demon called Kalma behind those doors and that they must extract blood from one of the concubines and place it inside the doors in a giant bowl for the demon to drink. The doors are only opened for a few seconds, but we could rush into the chamber when they are opened."

Lynton said, "Superstition is used to control people. That is what religion is all about – control. However, there is something in that cave alright. I saw the flames and heard a voice from the depths of the cavern.

Old Barbizon interjected, "I assumed those lead doors were there because of radiation, but perhaps there is something more sinister within that cavern."

They started on the short trek, purposefully leaving signs for their pursuers to follow, as she shared with them her plans to lure them into a bed of quicksand that lay on the periphery of the lake. Once trapped there, they would be rendered defenceless.

Before them in the now even darker night spread a vast open scrub forest of stubby small trees that grew almost to the foot of the cliffs and stretched downward to the shore of the lake, actually forming a landscape of exceptional pristine beauty glimmering in the flickering moonlight.

Lynton mentioned her hunger, so old Barbizon reached over to a nearby pear cactus, inserted his knife and pulled the fruit off the stalk. He reached down and grabbed a leaf, held the cactus with it as he carved it open, exposing the soft, juicy fruit. He handed it to Lynton, who somewhat hesitantly brought it up to her mouth.

Smiling, old Barbizon said, "It is actually very good – eat."

Much to her surprise, it was very tasty. She thanked him as he said, "I can smell our pursuers. They are no more than half a kilometre behind us."

Lynton said, "The quicksand to which I alluded is but a small walk from here."

The ordinary sounds usually go unnoticed, while a lesser sound, portending danger or suggesting the unfamiliar, may be more acute at times. It was a sound falling into the latter category that made young Barbizon place an ear against the ground. "They have a vehicle now."

Standing erect, his great chest rising and falling to his breathing, he listened intently, motioning for the others to be quiet. His sensitive nostrils, seeking to confirm the testimony of his ears, dilated to receive and classify the messages that the wind bore to him and now his father.

It is the business of the beasts and the men of the wild to know what their enemies do. Young Barbizon stretched his great muscles and moved down the nearby slope of the foot hills in the direction from which had come the evidence that their enemies were now in possession of a vehicle.

Danny took Lana by the hand and squeezed to let her know he would protect her. Never before in his nearly 40 years had he even approximated anything this close to love. She looked up at him and smiled, knowing that she had a protector.

Barbizon bounded back up and said, "They are coming fast, but they are all in an armoured vehicle now. If we can get that vehicle into the quicksand, we shall be free of them all at once. Quick Lynton, lead us to where the quicksand is."

The arrogance of Major Dunther was typical of those who revel in perceived superiority of rank and ethnicity that they believe somehow makes them invulnerable to the normal perils that afflict others. Now sitting atop the armoured vehicle, impervious to his vulnerability to rifle fire, so cocksure of the coming destruction of the small band, he threw caution to the wind.

Having circumvented the quicksand, all were now safely on the far side. In order to make sure their followers went into the quicksand, which was well-hidden in the dark, Barbizon and the rest of the band had climbed the far hill and rolled boulders down, which they logically assumed would make the vehicle pivot to the right and enter into the vast field of quicksand that was on the periphery of the lake.

They all assembled on the far side of the quicksand and waited anxiously for the arrival of the armoured vehicle. Once it came into view, they turned to act as if they were running.

The vehicle lumbered forward as Major Dunther shouted something in German. Reaching the spot on the trail where the boulders had been rolled onto the roadway, the vehicle pivoted to its right and trudged forward. At first, it slowed only a bit, but gradually became bogged down in the grime.

Realizing what was happening, Dunther ordered his men out. He scurried to the back of the vehicle. By then, Danny had squatted and taken aim. He did not have to fire at Dunther as when he stepped off the vehicle, he sank immediately into the quicksand. Begging and pleading for help, he was quickly sucked under as screams of desperation filtered out of the vehicle.

The armoured vehicle was helpless in the quicksand. What served as thick heavily leaded protection was actually a hindrance as the weight of the vehicle prevented it from getting out of the dark, dank, deep bog. Smoke bellowed out of the engine compartment as the driver kept trying to get it to move, but it was a hopeless effort. Suddenly, the engine bellowed smoke high into the night sky and the screams from within grew in intensity.

When the men tried to exit the side doors, they could not open them more than a few centimetres. The quicksand poured into the vehicle as it began to slowly sink. The driver and co-driver tried to open the overhead doors, but by then the doors were under the quicksand and they simply were overwhelmed, as the muck and mire poured in. Amid the screams, Barbizon motioned for them all to turn and walk toward their rendezvous with destiny, as that tapestry of fate was nearing completion.

Chapter 9

The Lesser of Two Evils

Himmler turned his grief into roses,
But he threw away the flower and kept the thorns.
It is hate that has consumed him,
And he shall forever wear horns.
The fire in the cave he found one day,
And he embraced it to survive.
The hate inside grows ever stronger.
It needs his wrath to stay alive.

People fear his presence,
As he embraces every disgrace.
This is evil loving darkness
Turned into hate without a face.
This wretched form of desolation
Has made him evil, bitter and cold;

Lynton's South African Adventure: Demon of Fire at the Karoo Escarpment

The loathing he now displays toward grace

A reminder of the soul to the devil he sold.

Danny would not let go of Lana's hand, as finally, after a lifetime, he had found something he treasured more than money. And how she clung to him, for she had brought out the soft side of a hard man. The worst of times can bring the best out in a person, and though he knew he might not survive, all Danny wanted was to see that Lana was able to live.

Lynton made them bear to the left at the base of the back of the mesa, pointing upward toward the area where she had emerged from captivity. As they climbed upward, young Barbizon reached back and gripped Lynton, pulling her up toward him. With her by his side, he reached over and put his arms around her, pulling her close, so that he would make sure she did not slip. His father looked on with delight, assuming that the two of them had found each other in this moment of harrowing despair.

Lynton's South African Adventure:
Demon of Fire at the Karoo Escarpment

Arriving at the opening, which at the point of entrance was rather large, Lynton pointed at it and said, "It is fine for about 100 metres, but then toward the chamber where a cauldron of fire burns in an abyss, the opening narrows to the point that no one much bigger than I can squeeze through."

Larry said to Lynton, "What really worries me are those doors." Then, he turned to old Barbizon and continued. "You are sure they will be opened at noon?"

"Oh yes, every day it is done like clockwork."

Lynton said, "Do not think me crazy, but I believe the doors are there to keep something at bay, something that is in the cauldron of fire."

Barbizon's father said, "She is right, there is something in that place, something in the abyss that they all fear. I am assuming it is a ploy used by Himmler to control his workers, but I must admit that it could be something more sinister."

Larry said, "What must be feared are the plans they have to remove those nuclear devices from the cave and wreck havoc on the world."

"As I said, they have a map with Fort Knox, Kentucky and the Federal Reserve Bank on Liberty Street in lower Manhattan circled, which can only mean one thing," offered Lynton.

Larry, nodding his head, offered an assessment. "Yes, once they set off these bombs, the radiation will render the gold supply useless for one thousand years at the very least, and the U.S. economy will collapse. According to our intelligence agents, a group of financiers, including one American billionaire, now control 40% of the gold market. This will put them in near complete control of the world's economy. We have only a short window of opportunity to see that these bombs do not get out of those caves."

Barbizon said, "I will check the opening. Stay here."

As they waited for his return, they all sat quietly, contemplating what they had to do. Barbizon emerged from the cave and said, as he pointed to Larry and Danny. Do not fire your weapons under any circumstances. Anyone shows up, you must dispatch them with any weapon that is quiet, because if they are alerted, it will not take them long to get over here." He then motioned for his father to leave with him as he said, "We'll be a few minutes." He then looked at an overhang and continued. "Gather up rocks and build a cauldron under that overhang. Start a fire under it, as we will need it very, very hot."

No one questioned the purpose. They just got to work doing as they were told. Within thirty minutes, the two Barbizon's were back with small bloodied and gutted wildebeests on their shoulders. They made a drain off the cauldron into an opening they dug in the ground and as the fat burned off the carcasses, young Barbizon said, "No time for embarrassment. All strip down and grease up. We will be able to squeeze through I am sure, but it is best that the smaller of us go first.

Lynton had no shame and started to remove her clothes almost immediately when Barbizon said, "Not necessary. You already have made it through and Lana is almost your size, so she will be OK, too. Danny and Larry, on the other hand, you need to strip down to your underwear. My father and I are already nearly naked. However, we should all cover ourselves with the fat renderings just to be sure."

Being the smallest, Lynton led the way into the land of forbidden darkness that engulfed her and the rest. In the abstract of the gloom, everything fell silent, as a light mist seeped into the long, winding corridor of fear. Slowly, the minutes crept by. The darkness became lighter as the opening in the chamber could now be seen.

As Lynton came to the tight part of the corridor, she breezed through it with ease, thinking to herself that maybe she had lost some weight during her desert sojourn. She almost chuckled when she thought of her Wayne often teasing her about dieting. He was always saying, "I'll make a fortune with Lynton's Cookie Diet, or Lynton's Pizza Diet, and now he could come up with a really good one, Lynton's Desert Diet."

She wiggled into the giant chamber and there on her right was the fiery abyss with flames shooting upward with a fury. There was a low rumbling sound coming from below and she moved to the left, toward the lead doors.

Lana crawled out, followed by two rifles thrust out into the chamber, then came Larry and Danny. The two Barbizon's were bloodied and scratched from scraping against the tight cave walls as they emerged, and the smell of all those there was extremely pungent from the grease and sweat.

All eyes focused on the flames soaring upward from the abyss to their right. Old Barbizon, ignoring the flames, looked to the doors and said, "We shall wait until noon, and then when the door is opened, we must rush out into the chamber." He pointed at Lynton as he took the gun from Larry and handed it to Lana. "I, my son, Lana and Danny will attack those guards and the civilians. Show no mercy. Mercy will get you killed. Lynton will lead Larry to the bombs while we do what we can to contain the guards and workers."

179

While the group gathered around, Lynton drew on the ground, with old Barbizon nodding in agreement, in regards to the location of the bombs.

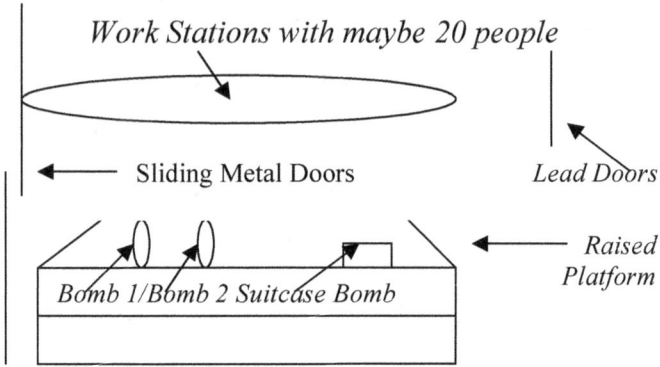

Work Stations with maybe 20 people

Sliding Metal Doors

Lead Doors

Raised Platform

Bomb 1/Bomb 2 Suitcase Bomb

"So," offered a confident Danny, "there really are no guards there?"

Lynton said, "No, they are in the adjacent corridor and spread throughout the caves."

Larry said, "We are at a critical point. I am sure the bombs are about to be loaded on a plane that, based upon the tail logo, belongs to a billionaire businessman from Manhattan, and he will be allowed to land in the USA without any inspection. From there one of the bombs will remain on his plane, and the other will be transferred to another plane."

Lynton interjected, "And the bombs will be dropped on the Federal Reserve Bank in Manhattan and on Fort Knox, obviously at the exact same time. It will be an air burst and the gold will be contaminated for a thousand years."

Larry nodded his head in agreement, and looked at his watch. "11:50 – almost zero hour. Are we all ready?"

They all prepared for the doors to be opened as they readied for a desperate attempt to save the world from a terror perpetrated by the intrinsic evil of greed from the billionaire and the equal evil of thirst for power as practiced by the ruler of Russia. This band of six brave souls was all that stood between the triumph of one form of evil in the name of power and greed, and the almost equally as abhorrent evil of the USA, a hypocritical nation that proclaimed itself the saviour of a world it wanted to control with its corrupt brand of corporate capitalism that made slaves out of working men and women so the elite might live in splendorous luxury.

Lynton thought to herself that justice rarely prevailed, because in the end, nothing ever came down to real justice, but rather a choice between the lesser of two evils.

Chapter 10

They Had Saved the World

This is the sorrowful story

Told as the twilight failed,

When the malicious one walked about

As evil on a sea of hate sailed.

'Twas when the rain of villainy fell steady

That the flames of hell came from below.

These brave minions feared not,

As into the breech they prepared to go.

Was Kalma a demon for real,

As in the pit one could hear

Murmurs of evil upward flowing,

But the heroes had no fear.

Lana staggered, her knees gave beneath her, and she sat down heavily a few feet from Lynton. Tears welled to the eyes of Danny as he went over and placed his hands on her shoulder. "Fear not little one, I shall protect you until my last breath."

She looked up at him and smiling, replied, "I know that."

Adversity often brings out the very best in people. Danny had spent his entire life on the edge of respectability, but never had any reason to grab hold of it. Now, this little native girl had made him want to grasp the hope of a normal life in the arms of someone who had brought out the best in him.

Lana looked into his eyes and said, "Don't die my love."

He quelled his emotion and was roughly wiping his eyes on his shirt sleeve. "I ain't dying. I got too much to live for."

Just then, as the door eased open, all of them stood to the left against the wall out of sight. Himmler himself, carrying the rounded pot of fresh blood, walked in and moved toward the now soaring flames from the abyss.

All a sudden, as he stood about to pour the pot of nubile female blood into the cauldron of fire, from behind, rushed old Barbizon, who with a mighty shove hurled him into the flames.

All there turned and rushed forward into the chamber, not bothering to close the door behind them or even noticing the small suitcase left sitting on the floor by the door. Standing in the chamber, ready to do battle, they were all in shock as the room was empty. Looking up at the platform, it was shockingly apparent that the bombs had been removed.

Larry said, "They are on the plane. They will be flown out. We must stop that plane."

They made their way toward the entrance, where they were met by a well-armed band of soldiers. Spreading in a great half circle, the soldiers sought to surround and head off their quarry, whose strategy they had guessed was to get to the plane. One of the soldiers said, "Halt, drop your weapons and raise your hands."

Severely outnumbered, there was little choice as old Barbizon said to his compatriots, "Drop your weapons. We cannot succeed."

Danny reluctantly placed his weapon on the floor, but he noticed Lynton was starting to flex her leg muscles in an awkward fashion.

While all this was going on, at the Russian capital of Moscow in his Kremlin residence, the President of Russia was enjoying the company of one of his many women friends. As he sat on the sofa with her in his arms, he said, "In only a few minutes now my billionaire friend will take off with something in his plane that will make me the most powerful man in the world. Come my sweet thing, come sleep with the soon-to-be emperor of the world."

She swooned at his boastful proclamation and kissed him long, hard and passionately, floating blissfully in the arms of a man who seemed in complete control of all that he surveyed, but the President failed to take one thing into consideration. He had left something very important out of the equation. He was not aware that in the Karoo there was also a little Filipino known as the dynamic dynamo.

Lynton's South African Adventure:
Demon of Fire at the Karoo Escarpment

Lynton had, at times, used her feminine charms in a seductive manner to manipulate men. It was something she was not particularly proud of, but like most women, she did enjoy the power of her sexuality. She noticed the soldier in charge was staring intently at her. His weapon, a Kalashnikov AK-47 was tilted downward. She had for years been a star volleyball player and an accomplished dancer and singer. She had long ago given the dancing up, but she still loved doing Zumba, and her taunt calve muscles were filled with spring and the energy of a jack-in-the box. She glanced over at both Barbizon's, who knew immediately what she was about to do, and they thought it too risky, but before they could shout, "no," she turned a quick summersault toward the soldier, locking his head in a vice-like grip with her strong legs while grabbing his gun. As she did, the others leaped forward toward the soldiers, catching them with such surprise that unarmed people would go on the attack that they only managed to get off a few ineffectual bursts from their weapons.

Danny, picking up his rifle as did Larry, opened fire, mowing down the soldiers with precision using rapid bursts of fire. Meanwhile, the dynamic dynamo had literally strangled the soldier to death with her mighty grip while firing effectively as she lay on her back with the vice like grip on the soldier who had made the mistake of admiring her fine form. Mowing down three other soldiers with the rifle, Lynton finally released her grip. Below, mass confusion ensued as soldiers started climbing up the hillside, making themselves easy targets for the now well-equipped band of interlopers.

The climbers knew they were at a disadvantage and began to retreat. At the far end of the runway, the plane's engines were roaring to life as it prepared to take off. Larry said, "Hopefully the bombs have not been fused, but regardless of the consequences, we must stop it here in this desolate place to prevent mass destruction in a populated area. Under no circumstances can that plane be allowed to take-off."

Lynton's South African Adventure:
Demon of Fire at the Karoo Escarpment

All there knew what Larry was saying. In order to prevent mass casualties in the USA, the only alternative was to risk a huge nuclear explosion in the isolated Karoo. All human wisdom boils down to these words: *sacrifice for others is the boldest act of a human.*

Life is a storm in which you bask in the sunlight one moment, and are shattered on the rocks of hopelessness the next. What makes a person extraordinary is what they do when that storm comes.

Lynton's thoughts were of her dear Wayne, and how he would be devastated if she were not there for him to worship and adore, for she had rescued him long ago from the depths of despair, and she could not help but let a small smile creep across her lips at how he would also deplore the fact she had died for the defence of a nation that he saw as the biggest terrorist nation on earth, but when he would reflect, he would realize she was saving many innocents who were also victims of America's culture of greed.

Wayne had taught her that there are two ways of seeing: with the body and with the soul. The body's sight can sometimes forget, but the soul remembers forever. How could she live with herself knowing she had not done all that was possible, not to save the damned gold, but to save all the innocents who would also be incinerated for the glory of a billionaire who was just one of the abominations created by the culture of greed.

Old Barbizon reached down and took some keys off the body of the soldier, tossed them to Lana and said, "To the slave chambers and release the women and Mantulu. Though they may only know freedom for awhile before we are all incinerated, let them grasp freedom again before they embrace eternity."

He then reached down and from one of the dead soldiers picked up a bandolier that was filled with grenades. "The plane will roar by here in a second, keep your firepower leveled at the soldiers below, and I will jump onto the plane's wing and blow it up."

Young Barbizon looked into his father's eyes and said, "No. I will do it."

Smiling, his father replied, "Son, chances are the bombs are already fused. We will all probably die anyway, but I am the oldest and have had life, a life that since losing your mother has known no joy except for you. I go in the hope you will live."

Larry interjected, "This is my job and none of you here are being paid to take this risk."

Lynton said, "It isn't about pay. It is about the sanctity of human life, and how these monsters have total disregard for that sanctity. We are here because we want to be, because we all share in our disgust for the maniacal worship of money and the belief in racial superiority that drives men to commit acts of barbarity."

Old Barbizon said, "Well put little lady. And that is why I go."

There was a lower ledge to the left of where they were. That ledge jutted out near the course the plane had to follow in order to take-off. Old Barbizon instructed them to concentrate fire to distract the soldiers below while he climbed behind the scrub to the ledge. Then, when they saw him leap downward onto the wing, they were to run as fast as they could into the interior of the cave to escape the blast.

Lana came back with the women and Mantulu, and they picked up guns, prepared to assist in the battle against evil. They squinted from exposure to the sunlight as they had lived in darkness for a long time. One of the women stared at young Barbizon and said, "I know you Lord of the Karoo. I am Fatima, who you once saved from a rhino attack when I was 12. I stand with you against evil."

Young Barbizon nodded in recognition and gave her a slight smile as his father came over and embraced him while saying, "I am proud of you my son."

Tears filled young Barbizon's eyes and he could find no words. He stood in awe of his father, who was about to give his life for those in a far away land who would, in all likelihood, never know of his sacrifice.

Barbizon gave the signal to begin firing. A fusillade of bullets rained down upon the soldiers who scrambled for cover. Barbizon skilfully moved behind a rock near the ledge and waited for the plane to roar past. The firings continued unabated as the plane started its takeoff. Popping the pins out of two grenades, with the rest in a bandolier around his shoulder, holding the trigger lock down in his hands, Barbizon prepared to make his leap. The fall would be a good 100 feet, but all he needed to do was land on the wing and let go of the trigger mechanism to cause the plane to explode, as he would be over the fuel tank.

Lynton's South African Adventure:
Demon of Fire at the Karoo Escarpment

In the plane, the billionaire eased back with confidence, already counting the billions he would make from this act of terrorism. He would avoid customs inspection because of who he was, and the bombs would be loaded on another aircraft while he hastily made his way to his 50 million dollar estate in Florida where his children awaited him. His third wife was still in New York, and he smiled as he thought getting rid of this one was easier then the other two. Ah, and his second ex-wife lived in Louisville, Kentucky, near Fort Knox, where the other bomb would explode. He eased back in his seat, smiling and ignoring the gunfire as his lackeys served their master with undying loyalty. He had never made any sacrifices for others in his life, having been handed 250 million dollars by his father to start his empire. He was one of the privileged classes who had the world laid before them on a silver platter. These money grubbers and hoarders of wealth were the new aristocracy, and the incredibly ignorant masses actually worshipped them.

The people with money thought they had wealth, but what they really had was poverty of the soul. This was a man the world would not miss. He built towering structures but they were monuments to his greed, not his intelligence. Can wealth give happiness? Look around and see the distress of those who are never satisfied with what they have. Whatever fortunes are accrued, the mind annihilates and calls for more. This was a man with no satisfaction in life, because what he got only filled a deep dark cavern within his soul that was bottomless.

Old Barbizon looked back at his son as he stepped out on the ledge, and with a smile on his face almost seemed to take flight as he dived downward toward the plane's left wing. Bullets from below tore into his flesh and blood spurted like a geyser, but he refused to be kept from his appointed destiny. He landed on the wing with a thud, letting go of the two triggers on the grenades, while up above, the others scurried into the cave as a mighty explosion thundered all about the Karoo. The soldiers below were engulfed in flames and as the plane smouldered, it was obvious from the lack of a mushroom cloud, that the bombs had not been triggered.

Lynton walked over to Barbizon and put her arms around him. She could find no words, but she needed none. They all walked out into the sunlight as the few remaining soldiers alive were quickly fleeing into the desert, where they would, no doubt, eventually die from thirst.

The woman saved by Barbizon so many years ago came over and took his right hand, looking up at him with sympathetic eyes that shared his pain. Lynton smiled, because she felt that the two of them might find love. She then looked over at Lana and Danny. Lana had given Danny something he had always needed – affection. And it had changed Danny from a bitter, hardened felon into a man of character.

They all walked down the side of the mountain with a sense of exhilaration. Hey, they had saved the world!

Epilogue

The Suitcase and Sewing the Threads of Evil

It is the way of weakened minds

To see everything through a black cloud.

The soul forms its own horizons,

And the darkness that abounds

May never be conquered,

But fear can indeed be vanquished.

Sometimes, the vanquished realize their errors, and for that reason, Agus came forward with his hands up and said, "Fool that I am, that I did not tear out my heart the day I resolved to revenge myself and others. I meekly offer my life for you to do with as you please."

Those there shrugged their shoulders, and Lynton said, "Go to your wife and children. Embrace them and be happy. The fight is over."

197

Lynton's South African Adventure:
Demon of Fire at the Karoo Escarpment

Often we pass beside happiness without seeing it, without looking at it, or even if we have seen and looked at it, without recognizing it. Lynton knew where her happiness lay. It was with Wayne back in Cape Town, so she bid goodbye to all her new friends and travelled back in a Land Rover with some military personnel who had showed up once word of what ensued got back to Cape Town. On the way back, she reflected on all that had transpired, but there was one thing that bothered her.

Yes, there had been a mighty victory over evil in the Karoo, and it was true that wealth without work, pleasure without conscience, knowledge without character, commerce without morality, victory without sacrifice had been laid waste in that plane which was now strewn all over the base of that evil mountain. She had once read that rich people had small televisions and big libraries and the poor people had big televisions and small libraries, but the truth was that the poor of the world could not afford big libraries any more than they could afford an education. Ignorance made them easy prey for the unscrupulous. That is why they so often voted against their own self-interest. The cards were stacked against the poor, but they could go to the public library for their knowledge, but that took effort, just as taking down the evil of Himmler took great effort. She and her compatriots could have shrugged their shoulders and given up. Had the evil just been perpetrated against the moneyed class and greed, Lynton may not have lifted a hand, but the problem was there were also many poor people in Manhattan and Kentucky. Their suffering she found untenable.

Throughout history, it has been the inaction of those who could have acted; the indifference of those who should have known better; the silence of the voice of justice when it mattered most that has made it possible for evil to triumph. Lynton felt good about herself, because she had refused to bow before evil, but still she had that slight doubt if she and the others had really triumphed, because there was that one lingering question that preyed upon her fertile mind, almost playing a symphony of doubt if there might have been something they overlooked. That is what gnawed at her insistently as the car made its way back to Cape Town.

There was that one question she needed answered. When Himmler had been hurled into the fire, there was no scream, and what of that abyss of fire? What was really down there? Suddenly, she remembered the suitcase bomb had been left by the door. She had seen it but never bothered to mention it as, in all the commotion to find the bombs, it somehow had seemed less important. She turned to the Colonel who was sitting with her and asked, "Did you find a suitcase by the large lead doors that shut off the abyss of fire in the back chamber?"

Surprised, the Colonel replied. "There was no abyss of fire anywhere in the caves, and no suitcase."

Lynton stared straight ahead and wondered about the legend of Kalma, Lord of the Underworld. Had she and the others been seeing things? Also, what of the flames that had soared upward from the abyss? Could there have been a ledge upon which Himmler fell rather than into the flames? After all, there were no screams. Could he have managed to crawl back up? Most of all, she wondered about that suitcase and the bomb that was obviously in it. Was that tapestry of fate still sowing the threads of evil?

The End or Is It?

Don't Miss These Exciting Lynton Adventures
By
J. Wayne Frye
(For Young Adults)
(1) Lynton Curls Her Hair
(2) Lynton Buys a New Cell Phone
And Hears the Voice of Doom
(3) Lynton Walks on Water
(4) Lynton and the Vampire at Tagaytay Manor
(5) Lynton Viñas and Beowulf Perez
Demon Fighters in the Taal Inferno
(6) Lynton and the Ghosts
At the Mansion on Balete Drive
(Lynton Adventures For More Mature Readers)
(7) Pursuit
(8) Lytnon Vinas:
Demon Fighter in Black and White
(9) Chablis and Lynton in the Room of Doom

Lynton's South African Adventure:
Demon of Fire at the Karoo Escarpment

Vocabulary (Farflex Canadian Dictionary)

Introduction (Page 5)

voluptuous - having a curvaceous figure

succulent - delectable

melancholia - persistent sadness or hopelessness

transgressions - to go beyond or over the law

equitable - just and fair

modicum - a small amount of something

chronicler -a person who tells a story (tale)

Prologue (Page 9)

grandeur - grand or magnificent

fathom - understand

deprivation - deprived of something (necessities)

irresponsibly - not being responsible

exploitation - taken advantage of

dictates - authoritative suggestion

siblings - brothers or sister or both

tenacity - persistence, extreme determination

arduous - demanding great effort - difficult

lingered - stay in place or slow in leaving

dissipated - lost/broken up

teeming - full, abound

vibrant - vigorous, lively, full of enegery

ethnically - related to ethnic category

fabulously - astonishing

dazzled - amaze, overwhelm

glistening - shine, sparkle with lustre

pall - to darken or obscure

beckoning - to summon or direct

brooding - depressed or moody acting

dampen - to restrain or depress

radiance - brightness or light

vibrancy - throbbing with energy, lively
trepidation - state of alarm or dread
luxuriously - great beauty or pleasure at great cost
disordered - confusion or disarray
debased - to lower in quality or value
intimidation - to fill with fear, to threaten
glistened - to shine brightly
cower - to crouch or cringe in fear
Chapter 1 (Page 15)
inglorious - disgraceful
notoriety - wide recognition for one's deeds
repulsed - disgusted, repelled
equitability - equal or fair
obscurity - unknown
traumatic - psychologically painful
trek - to travel slowly (usually with difficulty)
topography - the features or configuration
expansive – wide ranging
lucernes - alpha, pats or hay
cacophony - harsh sounds
sombre - gloomy, dark, dull feeling
abode - residence, dwelling
primal - first, original, as if in base instincts
eerie - uncanny fear, weird
nocturnal - relating to the night
majestically - majesty, dignity
stealthily - acting almost invisible, sneaky, unseen
acrid - sharp, stinking, bitter (usually smell)
ruddy - red or reddish
sheen - lustre, brightness, shine
nefarious - extremely wicked or villainous
Karoo - semi desert natural region of South Africa

escarpment - a long precipitous ridge of land
forlornly - lonely and sad
piqued - to excite or arouse
utopia - an ideal place or state
insidious - treacherous or deceitful
predominate - stronger or leading element
miniscule - very small
caldron - large kittle or boiler
charade - a deception
antagonism - hostility or opposition
Chapter 2 (Page 37)
fanatical - extreme zeal or enthusiasm
secularism - devoid of religion
Allah Akbar – God is great
Robo-tons - like a robot
apartheid - former rigid form of racial separation
destitute - devoid, completely lacking
aggrandized - to make great or greater
acquiesce - to submit without protest
servitude - slavery or bondage of any kind
manifestation - outward indication
solitude - alone
propensity – naturally inclined to something
invigorated - fill with life or energy
nubile - young woman sexually developed
devoid - without
demented - crazy, insane, mad
conjure - to call or command an evil entity
oblivion - gone and forgotten
uncanny - not able to explain, mysterious
sinewy - tough and firm
lithe - limber, supple, flexible

Lynton's South African Adventure:
Demon of Fire at the Karoo Escarpment

pulsate - to vibrate, quiver
premonition - a forewarning
voluminously - a great size
titillation - excite or arouse
foreboding - inner feeling of future misfortune
permeated - to saturate or pervade
disinterred - to exhume, dig up
catatonic - appearing to be in a daze, unresponsive
blasphemous - irreverent, profane
dank - humid, damp, chilly
despicableness - deserving to be despised
preposterous - beyond reason or common sense
cahoots - in partnership with
perpetrated - to commit, cause to happen
squalid - miserable, degraded
iconic - tradition
tranquility - peacefulness
retribution - revenge
writhe - to twist or squirm – usually in pain
abomination - vile, shameful, detestable
depravity - horrible, bad, evil, corrupt
sordid -dirty, filthy, corrupted
ambled - slow, easy pace
awe - overwhelming feeling of admiration or fear
propitious - favourable
delineation - to differentiate with precision
defile - to make foul, dirty, unclean
vehemently - strongly emotional, intense
denizen -adaptable person to a new situation
dalliance - amorous toying, flirting, spending time
predicated - to imply or assert
chagrin – feeling of disappointment

Lynton's South African Adventure:
Demon of Fire at the Karoo Escarpment

Chapter 3 (Page 71)

precipitous - extremely or impossibly steep
apparition - a spectre or phantom
demonology - study or belief of demons
Apocalypse - cataclysmic end of times
authenticity - genuineness
impediments - physical or mental barriers
spellbound - captivated, enchanted, fascinated
incredulously - sceptical
tenacity - persistence
rendezvous - a meeting
nefarious - extremely wicked or villainous
plausible - appearance of truth or reason
luminosity - enlightened, intellectually brilliant
anonymity - anonymous – not known
paragons - exceptional merit or excellence
unwittingly - unintentional, accidentally

Chapter 4 (Page 91)

tempest - violent disturbance or commotion
tumultuous - highly agitated, disorderly
clandestine - done in secrecy or concealment
thwarted - prevent from accomplishing
bulwark - protection against external danger
acquiescence - agreement or consent
conduit - a way of conveying something
finite - having bounds or limits, measurable
astute - clever, cunning, shrewd
impetuousness - rash action, emotion, impulsive
impetuous - impulsive

Chapter 5 (Page 109)

problematical - doubtful or questionable
scrutiny - close and continuous watching

euphoria - extreme happiness
accosted - to confront boldly without restraint
connoted - to suggest or signify
laboriously - much work or labour
discombobulated - confused, upset, frustrated
cretins – stupid, dumb person
Reichsfhrer – commander of the SS in Germany
Holocaust - mass slaughter, Jews large loss of life
occultism - belief in supernatural agencies
neo-pagan - contemporary form of paganism
vanguard - forefront in any movement (before)
mongrelisation - cross-breeding with the inferior
xenophobia - fear of foreigners or strangers
conglomeration - clustering, combining
adherents - a follower or supporter
promulgating - to declare or set forth publicly
anomalies - deviation from the common/abnormal
vindictive - inclined toward revenge
panacea - a cure all, a perfect solution
cataclysmic - violent upheaval
orgasmic - intense or unrestrained excitement
impediment - obstruction or obstacle
plundered - to take wrongfully
reconstitute - to reconstruct
Armageddon - last completely destructive battle
reconnoitre - to inspect, observe, survey
Chapter 6 (Page 131)
miscreants - villainous depraved persons
mayhem - random, deliberate violence obliteration
braggadocio - a boasting person, braggart
covetness - to desire without consideration
aura - a certain quality or air about a person

aberration - departing from the right, normal
scowl - gloomy threatening look
personification - person showing a certain quality
Chapter 7 (Page 141)
quagmire - soft ground difficult to get of
Beelzebub - name for the devil
ruse - a trick, fraudulent deception
crematorium - place for cremation
lair - a resting place, usually for a wild animal
riling - to purposefully try to upset someone
aperture - opening, hole, gap
prowess - exceptional ability at something
serpentine - a winding course
cache - hiding place for ammunition, treasure
conjecture - speculation
essence - basic real nature of a thing
Chapter 8 (Page 161)
adroit - expert or nimble in use of hands or body
steely - like steel
periphery - external boundary of an area
pristine - uncorrupted, unspoiled
acute - sharp, intense, severe
concubines - woman kept for sexual purposes
impervious - incapable of persuasion, not affected
circumvented - go around or bypass
Chapter 9 (Page 173)
wretched - despicable, corrupted, mean
pungent - sharp smell or taste, disgusting
perpetrated - to execute, carry out
intrinsic - the very nature of something
Chapter 10 (Page 183)
quelled - suppress, put an end to

interlopers - a person who interferes or meddles
bandolier - belt over shoulder with ammunition
maniacal - behaviour like a maniac
barbarity - brutal inhuman conduct
fusillade - continuous discharge of firearms
unabated - without stop
accrued - natural growth or addition
annihilates - completely eliminated
geyser - spew forth with force
felon - wicked person
Epilogue (Page 197)
untenable - incapable of being defended,
unscrupulous – no conscience or scruples